THE
DREAM
RUNNER

THE
DREAM
RUNNER
by Audree Distad

Harper & Row, Publishers

New York, Hagerstown, San Francisco, London

THE DREAM RUNNER
Copyright © 1977 by Audree Distad

Library of Congress Cataloging in Publication Data

Distad, Audree.
    The dream runner.

    SUMMARY: A young boy goes into the mountains to seek his inner
self in the manner of Indian boys of long ago.
    [1. Identity—Fiction] I. Title.
PZ7.D627Dr3   [Fic]   76-21389
ISBN 0-06-021684-0
ISBN 0-06-021685-9 lib. bdg.

For Allan

1

Sam heard about the vision quest from Clete—one of those handed-down stories that he liked best. The old man's recollections kept Sam company when he was alone, covering as many bare spots as the patches on his overalls.

They were taking a breather, sitting on the shady side of the livestock sales barn, around the corner from the sign:

WEED'S AUCTION—SALE EVERY TUESDAY
CATTLE, HOGS, SHEEP.

The boy, Sam, sat bunched up with his knees under his chin, his arms wrapped around them as though holding himself together. His thin face was solemn, but his blue eyes were wistful and eager. Strands of pale hair, usually like unruly dandelion fuzz, now lay pasted dark and wet against his forehead. He wiped the sweat under his nose against his shirt sleeve, but he could not erase the smell of the cattle pens.

Old Clete seemed crumpled in his work clothes. His short frame, worn thin, was sprawled along the ground. He blew out a long sigh and fumbled at the bib pocket of his overalls, pulling out a tobacco plug covered with lint.

"Blame near too dry to spit," he grumbled, tearing off a corner of the plug with his teeth. He chewed it, open jawed, cheeking it on one side where it bulged.

"That cud bobs like a fishing cork," said Sam. "Ever slides down your throat, you're a goner."

"Not today. This here heat'll get me first."

"Bet it's not the worst day you ever worked. . . ." Sam angled to hook one of Clete's stories. "Bet it was hotter on that cattle drive . . . or when you painted the water tower . . . or someplace else. . . ."

Clete let fly a streak of tobacco juice. "Nope. Today's the worst." His eyes closed and his face seemed to sag.

Not like Clete, Sam thought, not coming back with a story. Heat doesn't usually get him down. Sam rubbed his nose on his sleeve again. Lousy barn stink, he thought, wish I could go swimming right about now. "Clete," he said sourly, "we gotta finish cleaning pens today."

A wait and a slow reply. "They ain't going anywhere."

"But tomorrow's sale day."

The cud bobbled. "Yeah . . . they'll be dirty all over again." Clete tugged his straw hat lower over his face. Judging by the hat, he had done some spitting into the wind. "Don't pull that sober face of yours. We'll get to 'em."

"You going to sleep? You're looking to get fired." Sam checked right and left.

"Hah," Clete snorted. "Old man Weed's not apt to do that. There's no big line of people waiting for this job. Not ever'body's partial to cleaning out cattle pens, just you and me."

"I'm not partial to it!"

"Well, then, sit back. No sense rushing. Weed . . . he huffs and puffs, but he won't pester us today . . . way too hot."

"Can't argue with that," Sam said. "You could fry an egg on a shovel."

"Hmmph . . . it's hot enough to lay one hard-boiled."

Sam groaned. "How come you always do me one better?"

"Takes practice," Clete mumbled, "and age . . . old age."

"Age?" Sam echoed. "You told me you're just a spring chicken."

"I must of been lying," said Clete. "I woke up aged this morning, that's sure."

"Maybe it's the chewing tobacco," Sam said. "Maybe you're getting that locked jaw."

"What I'm getting," Clete muttered, "is a headache

from being pestered. Can't a man have some rest?"

Sam smiled. It felt good to tease Clete. Summer felt good. He didn't miss school with its days strung like so many barbs on a fence line. Where he sat shy of giving the wrong answer or saying the wrong thing. Some days he came away with such a heavy feeling his feet dragged. The only way he knew to shake it loose was to run. And he did. By himself, along a country road.

In winter he ran until the sun made an orange sheen on the snow crust. In spring, until the first streetlight blinked on. Even in summer, the running was his best time. Sam woke each morning eager to be out. The little heaviness that had followed him into vacation time was left behind when he ran. Then he felt light and happy and as if he could do anything.

"Sure," Sam said, "take a five-minute nap."

"Well, ain't you the soul of generosity. . . ."

There was no one in sight. Beyond the wooden corrals of the stockyard, heat shimmered and rippled over prairie grassland. Sam knew it wasn't water, but he liked the mirage. Once he'd seen the image of faraway mountaintops, hanging low in the sky, sharp and close. Ordinarily the peaks were only dark humps in the north, but some mystery of the air had floated them up that day, like a promise of things cool and high and inviting. Sam still remembered it whenever he wished he could be somewhere else. Which was often.

"Clete, you ever see things that aren't there?"

4

"Not lately," said his muffled voice. "People who do . . . general' get locked up." Then he chuckled as if he felt perkier. "That was a real short five minutes," he said. He patted the tobacco pocket and invited, "You want some?"

"Nope! Makes my mouth sour to think about it. How do you stand that stuff?"

"Shoot. Lets me shovel that dung like it was feathers." Clete fanned himself with his hat while his other hand scratched through his dark hair.

"Why . . . a little tobacco's good. My old Indian granddad used to loan me a puff of his pipe now and then. Fixed it with a little kinnikinnick. Claimed it'd help me grow."

"He must of misjudged," said Sam, still hoping for a story. "You're only about an inch higher than me."

"But I'm way tougher, so don't get sassy."

They lapsed back into silence. The heat, even in the shade, was discouraging. Sam pulled his sweaty tee shirt away from his chest and flapped in some air.

"Clete, did you really have an Indian granddad?"

"I did. A Sioux. You mean in all this time I never told you about him? Why, I learned to walk hanging on to his trouser leg . . . tagged after him ever'where he went. He had that Indian way with kids . . . can't remember he ever hollered at me. He wasn't a tall man either, come to think of it . . . but he seemed big enough to me. . . ."

Sam sighed as he listened. "I never had a granddad to tag after," he said.

"I had one of the other kind, too," Clete went on. "Different tribe. Called themselves Swedes." He shook his head. "Funny how that works. I been called a dumb Indian often enough, but I never been called a dumb Swede." His blunt face wrinkled with a grin as he looked up at Sam. "You want to even things out for me?"

"Nope," Sam said. "I wouldn't call you a name."

"Now, now, I wasn't charging you. Don't you ever fool with your friends? Make up nicknames and such?"

"No," said Sam in a low voice. Not counting some names he had been called. "Names aren't fair."

"Oh, don't go looking for 'fair' . . . you're not apt to find it," said Clete. "But, now, if I was to call you the 'blue streak,' you wouldn't get mad, would you?"

Sam guessed what was coming.

"I've seen you," Clete said, "plenty of mornings . . . out churning those long pony legs of yours along the road. One way and then the other. You never seem to get settled. What's all that for?"

"I like running." Sam grinned. "It's the best thing I do."

"You figure to be another Billy Mills, that Oglala runner?"

"I'm not near that good."

"Shoot, he didn't start out at the Olympics. He kind of snuck up on 'em, same as you." Clete shot out another stream of tobacco. "He must come of old Indian runners. You know, some could run all day . . . strong as mustangs. Yeah, I bet . . . you're an Olympic champ coming up."

"Sure, that'll be the day." Sam ducked his head and blushed. He didn't run for prizes. He never pictured himself winning any. That was for other people, people he only heard about.

Clete sighed. "I swear, Sam, I think if you were a butterfly, you'd walk to spite yourself. You got to step up and show your stuff."

Sam only shrugged in confusion.

"Well, if I'm not going to have any Olympic champ to brag about," Clete went on, "how about going into ranching with me . . . seeing how we're starting at the bottom in the cattle business. . . ."

Sam knew Clete's old joke. It usually made the boy sad. Angry, too, when the buyers laughed at it. For all the joking, Sam figured Clete did dream about a ranch, anything from a section to thousands of acres. Wasn't right to let folks laugh at it. Ought to keep quiet about what you want, Sam told himself, especially if there's not much chance of getting it.

But for now Sam went along with the joke to encourage Clete. "Ranching . . . I guess. Seeing how we're acquainted with cattle." He leaned forward as if to say, make it up for me. Make it as pretty as that mirage out there. "Where should we have it, you think?"

Clete seemed to lapse again. His eyes took on a lonely stare and his voice came out empty, reluctantly. "Somewhere cool and shady . . . with a cottonwood tree to stretch out under . . . and a deep-water stream comin' down from the mountains . . . and a range of wild hay. . . ."

It took Sam by surprise. "Yes," he said. He could almost believe it when Clete didn't joke about it. Now it sounded important, like a special dream.

The old man sat up abruptly and squared the hat on his head. "Shoot," he said, "there's no place like that. Not now, if there ever was. Least I never found none. Maybe you'll do better."

He spat tobacco juice and wiped the corner of his mouth with a red bandanna. As an afterthought he swabbed his forehead and the back of his neck, too.

"Aw, sure, Clete. We'll have a great place. We could start buying cattle tomorrow at the sale. How about it? Maybe some little Hereford calves. I'm partial to those little white-faces."

The wad in Clete's cheek worked down and up. "Shall we stake 'em out in your backyard or mine? Your momma thinks none too high of me as it is. If I herded cattle into her backyard, she'd have me arrested either for rustling or littering."

Sam laughed in relief, finding Clete back in form. "She might holler some, I guess."

Clete chuckled and shook his head. "It wouldn't be a right thing to do to the poor woman . . . trouble she's got bringing you up. Your momma wouldn't thank me putting ideas in your head. She don't appreciate me anyhow is my guess."

Sam kept quiet about his mother's opinion of Clete.

"We'll hold off the cattle buying," Clete went on, "till we got the proper spread. That's the tricky part anyhow, 'cause like I said, I never have found the right place at all. Maybe if I'd gone on one of them vision quests, like my granddad told me, that would have put me on the right track. Might have found some magic power to help me."

Sam felt a story coming. "What are they?"

"They? Who?"

"Those vision quests . . . "

"Ah . . . it was what old-time Indians believed. Talk about seeing things that aren't there . . . they put great stock in visions . . . to give them power, sort of help them over the rough spots."

"Power?"

"Kind of magic, you might call it. Not muscle power, exactly, but inside power. Backbone, so to speak. They knew it'd be there when they needed it."

"How'd they get the visions? Was it a ceremony?"

"Sort of a test, you could say. Most boys went

through it when they were about your age, I guess. How old are you?"

Sam straightened. "Thirteen . . . pretty near."

"Somewhere around there. When a boy was old enough, the medicine man'd lead him out of camp, off to a hill, high up. And he'd sit the boy down facing north. . . ." Clete paused. "I think it had to be north. Anyway . . . that boy stayed there all alone . . . with no food or water . . . for three days and nights. . . ."

"Nothing at all?"

"Not a thing. He was to sit and wait for a vision. Me, I'd a seen fried eggs and hash browns, but an old-time Indian boy, you see, he hoped some spirit would show itself and give him its power so he could act bravely. It was a kind of initiation from being a boy into being a man."

"And then what?"

"Ain't that enough?"

"No," said Sam, "you gotta tell me the rest of it. What'd the spirit look like?"

Clete sighed. "I should of never started this story with you. You're worse'n a dog hanging on a bone. You got to remember it's been a long time since I heard this, and my granddad wasn't such a spring chicken when he told it to me either, so between the two of us, we forgot a powerful lot."

"What you remember then."

"Don't rush me. I haven't thought about this for years. Sure appealed to me when I was little. Anyway, that boy sat there on top of the hill, and for him that was the center of the world. What he saw around him was the hoop of the world. Sometimes they called it the 'sacred hoop.' He sang songs to the spirits and gave up his prayers to the Great Mystery. That's how they called it, *Wakan Tanka*, the Great Mystery."

"And what about the vision?"

"That's what he was hoping for. Mostly it would be in the shape of some animal that came to him and talked to him, or taught him a song, or showed him some special thing for his medicine bag . . . to bring him power. That spirit was supposed to be his spirit helper . . . to call on when he needed power. After the three days was up, the medicine man collected the boy and led him back to camp. The boy told his vision so it could be explained. Usually he got a new name according to whatever his vision was. Made him one of a kind."

"What's it look like, you suppose?"

"Oh, I guess it's close to being a dream."

"Did your grandfather ever have one?"

Clete studied the distance for a moment, considering. "I don't know," he said slowly, "there was troubled times when he was a boy. The government was roping off the reservations and putting down the Indian ceremonies, except when they sneaked in one the government didn't hear about. But otherwise they were pretty much cut off from the way they'd been living.

"I guess my granddad knew about the vision quests from the old people. Sometimes I used to wonder . . . he could make it sound so real. He had a name, Alvin Running Moon, but I never knew if it was a vision name . . . or if he earned it in some special way as a boy . . . never know now. A man ought to know . . . but I don't."

Sam let the story float in his mind. From being a boy into being a man, that'd be something. Being your own self . . . one of a kind . . . finding your own power. The possibilities grew.

"Suppose I could do that?" he asked suddenly.

"What?" Clete was yawning.

"Go on one . . . a vision quest."

A snort of amusement. "What for?"

"I could use some magic power. Some days I don't seem to count for much."

Clete groaned. "I'm gonna call you Sam Many Troubles. You ache where you ain't even got muscles."

Sam straightened up at that, frowning, and stretched his long legs out before him. His scuffed shoes reminded him of the work waiting. The heat and heaviness washed over him.

As if sensing Sam's mood, Clete said, "Oh, I don't say it wasn't as good a way as any to grow up, getting hitched to some vision idea, wanting something magical. But you still got to add the sweat by yourself. Me, I've done plenty of sweating, but it didn't amount to a hoot." He slumped back and drew the hat over his eyes.

"Aw, Clete, don't say that."

"I already did."

"It sounds like science fiction or another planet . . . all those visions," Sam said.

"It does, in a manner," said Clete drowsily, "but, shoot, they lived right around here. Up north by the mountains you can still see tipi rings from a camp. Plenty of dreams and magic in those mountains, you bet." His voice trailed off.

Sam thought of his mountain mirage. It was almost a vision, he decided, except it didn't give me any power.

"Maybe we should go up and see those tipi rings sometime," Sam said. There was no response, so he tapped Clete on the shoulder. "How about that?"

"Not today," Clete mumbled. "I'm uncommonly tired today. Don't need vision dreams so much as sleeping ones. Gimme time."

"Okay," Sam said. He stood up and moved away so as not to bother Clete. The vision story was still in his mind, and the rippling image still washed low against the prairie. Wish it was a real lake, he thought, so I could take a swim.

No . . . be better if it was a vision . . . to help me

over the rough spots . . . make me strong as a daylong runner. That'd be a wonderful magic.

2

Sam eyed the long rows of pens waiting to be cleaned. There wasn't a sliver of shade in any one of them. Be like baking a bug in a bottle, he thought.

In some pens, stock, already delivered, was waiting for sale. The cattle bunched together, dusty, rearing their clumsy heads, eyes rolling, tails flopping at the flies. Sheep riled up puffs of dust as they pivoted back and forth, stiff legged. Only the hogs lay flat out.

Those animals look miserable, Sam thought, better check their water troughs. They'll be after water.

His own throat was scratchy dry, and just thinking of work made him hungry. His lunch bucket was empty, but there was always the cafe and Mina's homemade pie. He would not wait to eat it there, he decided, but take it along and get back to the watering. He walked with long, loose strides, straight-backed like a runner. The more he thought of the pie, the faster he went.

In the narrow lunchroom at the front of the sales barn, Mina was filling sugar shakers. She wiped her hands on a dish-towel apron and smiled at Sam as he came in. "Hi, handsome!" Her big voice fairly bounced off the shiny counter and the chrome coffee maker and the plate-glass window. "Want your usual? Banana cream?"

Two truck drivers, seated at the counter, looked around at Sam and laughed. Sam tried to grin, but his face felt stiff. "It's the best," he managed to say. He slid onto an empty stool and drained the glass of water Mina plunked before him.

"All my pies are good," Mina announced, "just ask me!" She dished a frosty slice onto a paper plate and slid it across the counter to Sam. "And free for my fans," she said with a wink. Then in a louder tone, "I'll over-charge some trucker."

"Thanks, Mina." Sam scooped up the plate and beat it outside to enjoy the treat.

He folded down the rim of the paper plate and bit into the cool, juicy custard. Delicious flavors trickled through his mouth. That Mina can sure cook pies, he thought. He took an enormous bite and got meringue on his nose.

"Hey, Sam, how's the job? I hear you're really clean-ing up."

The pie went sour in his mouth. No mistaking that voice. He had heard it over his shoulder all year at school. Sam, let me see your math paper. Hey, did your mom make that shirt? How come your face gets so red?

What's he doing here, Sam wondered. Hasn't he got

anywhere better to go? Slowly Sam turned and saw Denny steering toward the barn on a shiny, yellow bicycle.

"How about this," he called, backpedaling smugly, "brand-new, ten speeds! Beats running, Sam."

"Nice," said Sam, choking up the only word that occurred to him. Behind Denny was Bud, another classmate.

"Hot day to be working," Bud said as he stopped. He wiped his hands dry on his tee shirt, under the motto T.C.H.S. BOBCATS.

"We're working, too, aren't we?" Denny demanded. "We just delivered a prescription to old Mrs. Elwood. Pills to the pill."

Sam wiped the meringue away with his hand. His shirt was stuck to his chest and the pie began to dribble down his arm. One day they rode by without even waving, he reminded himself. Why'd they have to see me today? Wish I was back cleaning the pens. Don't say anything dumb.

"I gotta hand it to you, Sam," said Bud, "slaving away today. My dad wanted me to wash the car, but I ducked out."

"Sam doesn't mind," Denny put in, "he just loves cows and working here in the great outdoors." He wrinkled his nose. "Pheweeee . . . don't you wish the wind would come up?"

Sam shifted from one foot to the other. Clete joked

about the work, but it sounded different coming from Denny. Sam tried too hard to think of something to say and nothing occurred to him.

"Standing there holding that pie, you look like a wooden Indian," Denny said, grinning. Bud scowled and scuffed his foot over the gravel. "That's what comes of working with that old guy Clete," Denny went on. "Hey, does he ever take off that filthy hat?"

Sam wanted to throw the pie in Denny's face. "Clete and I get along fine," he said. "He works hard." Remembering that Clete was asleep in the shade, Sam glared at Denny as if he expected an argument.

"Oh, you got your spurs on," Denny laughed. "The old bum is your best buddy, huh? Heap friend?"

"He's not a bum!"

"Knock it off, Denny," said Bud.

But Denny continued to grin, enjoying the angry blush on Sam's face. Sam drew back stiffly and raised his chin.

It was Bud who changed the subject. "Are you going out for track this fall, Sam? My dad asked me, 'Who's that long-legged kid I see running?' I told him about you. You know my dad, don't you? The coach?"

Sam was so riled at Denny he barely nodded in Bud's direction, but Bud went right on talking. "You still run every day?"

Sam nodded again.

"How about if I come by and run with you. Be good

training for me . . . for football. I'd keep you company, too. Wouldn't you like that?"

Sam hesitated. Running didn't need company. It let him feel good about being himself. He wasn't sure he wanted it turned into training for football or track. Bud can come around and talk some, he thought, if he wants to be friends. Why does he have to butt in on my running?

"I go early," he said, "while it's cool. Around six."

"In the morning!"

Denny let out a long "Hoo, hoo! A whole cheering section couldn't get Bud up that early."

"It's cool then," Sam repeated. "I run out to the dam south of town and get back in time for work."

Bud fiddled with his handlebars. "That's three miles out, isn't it?" he said, sighing. "Well, Dad says I need to get into shape. I'll try, but . . . ah . . . don't wait if I'm not there."

Denny wheeled his bike around. "Let's not wait here either. Put your poor old three-speeder in gear, Bud, and let's go take a swim."

"Yeah," said Bud, "gotta practice my butterfly stroke. See you, Sam. Don't work too hard."

"Nope."

Sam did not watch them go. He looked down at his pie, now sagged out of shape by the heat and dripping off the sides of the plate. Just like me, he thought, all squishy and dumb. He dumped the pie into a trash barrel.

I've known those two since third grade, he thought, and I still can't talk up to them; it's like we used different languages or something. Old Bud acts like a king doing you a favor. How's he expect to run carrying all those baggy muscles?

Sam snatched up a spading fork from behind the barn and kicked open the gate of a pen. Denny thinks he's so funny. "I hear you're really cleaning up," Sam mimicked. And there he sits on his ten-speed bike. Be soft, having a ten-speed, or a three-speed . . . or any bike.

Thinking that made him feel mean. He knew his mother couldn't afford a bicycle. His own money would buy school clothes, except for his new running shoes. Pure foolishness, his mother had said.

He stabbed angrily at the bedding straw and came up with an empty fork. No good getting mad, he told himself, just makes extra work. He slid the thick tines carefully under the straw, catching a tangled nest which clung to the fork long enough to be deposited in a wheelbarrow. When that was full, Sam emptied it onto a larger waste heap behind the pens, trailing wisps of loose straw as he went.

Sam shoved open another pen. Where's Clete? Ought to be here helping me, Sam thought, not off sleeping. He bent to his work, scooping and pitching. It wasn't heavy but the sun was hot, and he wiped his head against his sleeve again and again. In the next pen a cow chewed calmly and watched him through the fence.

"Well, what are you looking at?" Sam muttered. "Never seen anyone work before?" Just like Denny, he thought, same expression. No, not fair . . . that cow looks smarter.

Old Denny couldn't even get to the dam and back riding his bicycle, Sam thought. How does he get off calling anyone else a bum? Bud and Denny wouldn't hang around Clete long enough to hear "Good morning," let alone a story about dreams and visions. They'd think it was silly.

Sam straightened and looked across the distance to the dark shadows of the mountains against the horizon. Dream mountains, he scoffed. Maybe for someone else. Not likely I'd find any magic there. My vision'd likely be a pitchfork. Seems like I'll be shoveling the rest of my life. Oh, come on, Sam, he argued with himself, stop whining. You're going to be an Olympic champ. Clete says so. Hah! Clete and his stories. Where'd they ever get him?

Sam's neck ached and the fork handle slid in his sweaty hands. On the second trip the wheelbarrow slipped and spilled sideways. Sam kicked at the mess, then he had to reload it. He was cleaning his fourth pen alone when Clete peered over the top of the wooden fence, smiling impishly.

"Oh, there you are, Sam."

"Where'd you think I was?"

"Oh, off someplace . . . maybe filling up on Mina's pie." Clete shoved back his hat and scratched his head. "You see my pitchfork?"

"About five pens back."

"That so? Well, save me some work while I go get it."

Clete's slump-shouldered, bowlegged frame rocked as he ambled off. It was several minutes before he returned with the fork. He stopped, braced against it. "Did I ever tell you about the time after the war when I was on that big cattle drive? Herded six hundred head from Killdeer to Billings. I ever tell you about that?"

"Ten times at least," Sam snapped. He was tired and still sore about Denny. Any more stories, he thought, and I won't get home for supper. That pie didn't exactly fill me up.

"I did?" said Clete. "Getting so old I repeat myself. Let's see, must be something you ain't heard about."

Sam's fork dug into the ground so hard it hurt clear to his shoulders. "What I never heard," he blurted, "was a man who blabbed so much. Do you get paid for talking or sleeping around here?"

Instantly he was sorry. Taking his temper out on Clete didn't help, especially seeing the old man's face.

"Clete, I didn't mean that," Sam stammered. "I always say the wrong things." Always, always, he thought savagely. "I like your stories. Don't I tease you to tell 'em? Go on . . . the one about the cattle drive to Billings."

Clete turned away and all Sam heard was his low voice. "It was nothing but a bunch of dirty riders shooing a bunch of dirty cows." The old man shuffled toward the gate. "Let's bring up some fresh hay."

Sam followed, silent and miserable. They lifted the bales of hay between them, hefting by the binding wires. Sam wore old cotton work gloves, but the wires weighed on his fingers like knives. While they worked he tried to think how to make it up with Clete. Every bale seemed heavier than the one before, and it was all he could do to handle his share.

"These miserable big bales," Sam puffed, "bet they'd make a hundred pounds or more."

"Close enough," Clete agreed, straining. "Any one'd outweigh you." He eased his end of the bale onto the ground with a sigh. "Be easier taking the cows to the stack . . . you carrying the cow and me bringing up the tail."

Sam dropped his end and laughed. It felt so good to laugh that he overdid it, collapsing against the wooden corral.

Clete plopped down hard on the bale to catch his breath. "So . . . Sam Many Troubles can still laugh," he said gently.

Sam tried to speak, but Clete waved his hand vaguely to head him off. The old man patted his bib pocket and frowned. "Could of swore I had some tobacco left, but it appears I am cleaned out . . . yup . . . cleaned out flatter than old Albert." He searched the pocket again. "I ever tell you that one about Albert?"

Sam frowned and shook his head.

"Must be all that talking about the visions," Clete said, "put me in mind of another Indian custom.

"There was this man I knew, name of Albert High Elk. And one day Albert took a notion to go on down to Parmalee with a friend of his, Billy Deale. So they hopped into Billy's pickup and took off without more'n a good-bye wave to Albert's wife, Leah. Well, late that afternoon, word came back to town that Billy's pickup was found on the road home wrapped all the way around a telephone pole. They figured to have to cut the bodies out." Clete wagged his head regretfully, and Sam's soft mouth wrinkled down at the corners.

"Now sometimes when an Indian died, they mourned him by burning all his things. And so, Leah dragged out ever'thing Albert owned—which wasn't so much—she hauled it out into the yard. His hammer and his spare shirt and such. Piled it all up and lit it afire. And then she commenced to sing and mourn over her dead husband."

Clete scratched his head while the boy waited. "Just about time the fire died down to a heap of red coals, here comes Albert walking down the road. Turns out he rode home with someone else and never was in the pickup at all. Well, sir, he didn't have much when he left that morning, and he didn't have but the clothes on his back when he got home."

Sam had to laugh, and the old man smiled as he would each time he repeated it. "Cleaned out flat," he said.

"Shoot, feels like mealtime, Sam. You go on home, your momma's waiting supper on you. I'll get these last bales." Clete braced his hands on his knees and haltingly stood up. Sam put out a hand to help him, although it wasn't like Clete to need it.

"Go on," Clete said, shooing him away. "Go on. You think I can't do this without you? Why, we just keep you on here to see you stay out of trouble." He nodded and grinned.

"I think I better stay. Won't take long to finish."

"What are you, some smart kid that won't take a hint? I'm telling you to beat it on home. Weren't you working while I was snoozing? Go on now, before I run you off."

Sam laughed. "See you tomorrow then, Clete."

"Bet you will. Get here bright and sassy. None of that sleeping till noon on a sale day."

Sam scuffed wearily along the road which led past the stockyard and toward his home. In spite of Clete's lively story, Sam realized the old man had been extra tired. I didn't help any by snapping at him, Sam accused himself. Maybe he's been working too hard. It's hot and he is pretty old. Tomorrow I'll work extra hard, take some of the load off. Let him have a chance to jaw with the truckers and buyers . . . he likes that. I'll try to make it up to him tomorrow . . . with the herding and watering. . . .

Watering! Sam stopped short, slapping his palm against his forehead. "I forgot!" he said aloud. I never did check the water in those troughs.

He half turned; he was almost home. Should I go back? he thought. Probably Clete will check. He surely will. Oh, I ought to go back . . . but Clete'll do it. Sure he will, he's not some dumb kid. Sam, you dope! First you holler at the old man and then you slack off on your own work.

He continued homeward, but the heavy feeling settled over him. That Denny, he thought, everything started going wrong when he showed up. I got so mad . . . and . . . course it wasn't Denny's fault either. I was the one who forgot the troughs, and I was the one who shot off my mouth.

His steps dragged as he approached the old, two-room house. There was nothing there to cheer him up, he thought. Lately it didn't seem to fit him any better than his old green coat, which bound at the seams and stopped short of his wrists. Must be me that's all wrong, he thought.

Sam pulled the catch of the wire gate. It squeaked when he pushed it open and it clanked shut behind him. In the north, the mountains were fragile and golden in the soft light. And far away. Maybe his mom would enjoy the story of the vision quest . . . if he told it so she could see that boy . . . sitting smack in the center of the hoop . . . with the world around him. If she would only, for once, listen to him.

3

Inside the house, light from the setting sun streamed through a window. It colored the edge of the faded blue curtains; warmed the arm of the brown, scratchy sofa, which was Sam's bed; and fell in a square at the base of the wobbly metal floor lamp. Gloom settled everywhere else. The screen door bumped Sam into the room.

"Why don't you turn on a light, Mom? Getting dark out."

"I can see all I want to. Spuds aren't much to look at. How do you want them—fried or boiled?" She leaned against the sink, peeling potatoes, her tall, raw-boned figure stooping over the work.

Sam wished she would turn and smile, as if she was glad to see him, but she seemed lost in thought, head bowed.

"Make 'em any way that's easy," he said.

"You're late, aren't you? Anything wrong at the sales yard?" Now she did peer at him, her eyes sharp and direct. Her high, round cheeks, usually a ruddy tone, were pale, Sam thought, but maybe it was the light.

"Be sure you do what's expected of you. Do your job." Her voice carried a twang that sometimes slipped into a whine. "Don't spend so much time on that Clete. You do just what you're told. You hear?"

"Don't start in on Clete."

"Well, he's no kind of pattern . . . you ought . . ." Her voice faltered and the paring knife dropped from her hand into the sink.

"Mom, I do my job. Mr. Weed wouldn't keep me if I didn't." Except today I wasn't so smart, he admitted to himself. Why was she carrying on so? "Don't fuss about me so much."

She sighed. "Oh, I know you do your job, I just . . . Have you thought to ask Mr. Weed if he'll keep you on this fall? Seems there must be jobs you could do there after school. The money'd be a help."

Sam sagged against the doorframe. She would pick then, he thought, after school when the kids play baseball on the field. Not enough me working all summer while everyone else goes swimming, now she wants me to work after school.

"Wash up and change. Hang those overalls outside on the line. Hurry up, now. I've plenty to do."

What now? Sam wondered. She's already cleaned house once this week. Wish Bud had asked me to go swimming today. I'd have gone, work or no work. I'm sick of having to do what I don't want to.

His mother spoke, but Sam was too sunk in his own thoughts to hear, until he felt her looking at him, intently. Her eyes were so dark and somber they startled the boy.

"What?" he asked.

"I said, I'll be packing after supper. I'll be gone for a few days."

"Where?" he asked, astonished.

But she motioned for him to hurry, her lips pressed tight, and turned back to the stove, slamming down a pan as if she aimed to break it.

Sam washed at the kitchen sink, scrubbing suds up past his elbows and then over his face and neck. He pulled clean blue jeans and tee shirt from the tall, painted dresser in his mother's room. Changing clothes, he tried to guess what had happened. There wasn't anywhere for her to go that he knew. It made him edgy, this mystery.

He set out thick white plates and coffee mugs on the table, glancing at his mother's back from time to time as though it could tell him where she was going. She dished up the food and sat down without a word. Everything about her expression was grim. Sam eased into his chair quietly, not slouching, and waited.

"Your father's sister called," she said. "Seems he

turned up in a hospital out on the coast and died there two days ago."

Sam's stomach lurched. It's not possible, he thought, there's no such person.

"She thought we ought to know they were bringing him home to bury him," his mother said.

No such person, Sam repeated to himself. How can he be dead? He wasn't ever alive. Not for me.

"I told her right out," his mother was saying. "I don't owe him anything, leaving me with a young child. I don't owe him. There wasn't much she could say to that."

Sam tucked his hands under his legs to keep them from shaking. He didn't know why they were shaking; it wasn't as if he had known his father. He was no more than a tall, skinny shadow Sam remembered from somewhere. It wasn't like a father who was a coach or bought bicycles. But Sam's hands continued to shake. He thought it shouldn't matter after all this time.

He hadn't asked much about his father, not since one particular afternoon when he was four or five, out playing in a ditch with Red and Elmer and Patsy. He remembered all their names and Patsy's pink hair ribbons and the smell of drying leaves in the ditch.

"Your dad is a bum," Red told him, "my folks say so."

"That's right," chimed Patsy. "He's a bum."

"What's that?" Sam had asked.

"Ask your mom. She'll tell you. Say is your dad a bum."

Sam never forgot the look on his mother's face. And he never asked again. After that he kept his hurts and questions to himself, and they floated beneath the surface, secretly, like blind fish in a dark pool.

And in other towns he covered the empty place with stories, one after another. "He died in a mine explosion . . . fighting a war . . . flying a plane." Generally it stopped the teasing, but if it didn't, Sam turned away and was quiet and told himself it didn't matter. Only now he could say "He's dead," and that would be enough because it was true.

"Still, I suppose it's only the decent thing," he heard his mother saying, "to go to the funeral. At least I can do the decent thing."

Why? Sam wondered. You never even say his name. We act as if nothing was wrong. "He left," Sam burst out. "He didn't ever come back. You don't owe him; you said so. Why do you go?" Sam didn't like the feeling that his mother was leaving him, too.

She leaned her elbows on the table and propped her head against her rough, chapped hands. Her voice sounded far away and soft. "He was young," she faltered, "young enough to run away. I guess he felt trapped here . . . with us. He wanted to be on the go, he used to say, not stuck in some jerkwater town. He sent us money a couple times; he did that. Once from Alaska . . . so I guess he had some jobs here and there. Maybe he even thought to come back and was too scared. . . ."

Sam sat rigid with anger to see his mother so sad. How many times had he tried to put a face on that shadow? He didn't want one now. "What was he scared of?" Sam demanded. "He shouldn't have gone. I don't care if he is dead."

His mother lifted her solemn eyes, but Sam looked away. He wasn't sorry for saying it. He felt shoved aside. As if the shadow had closed him out of his own house.

"I suppose not," she said slowly, "he didn't leave you much. Except . . . sometimes . . . when you forget yourself and let loose a big grin . . . then you look like him. Your floppy hair is like his. Rest of the time you keep yourself so quiet and so . . . watchful. I wish I could help you sort it out, Sam. But I guess you'll have to make your own sense of it."

Sam stared blindly at the bare wall with a tightness growing inside.

"You'll be all right, staying alone for a few days?"

His throat hurt. His mouth drew down defiantly. "I've done it before."

"I know. I depend on you, Sam." She made a half gesture as if reaching toward him, then hesitated and rose from her chair, leaving her food untouched. "Will you clean up? I haven't much time." She took a slow look around the room, as a stranger might have. "Not much of a house," she said, "when you look close. We meet ourselves coming and going. I wish it was different for you."

"It's okay," Sam said stoutly. "I like it just fine." Not always, he remembered. He was frightened, feeling so alone. Too much had happened too quickly. He didn't want his mother to go and yet he wanted to help her. "You want me to go, too?"

She shook her head. "Costs too much. You never knew him. I'll see it finished proper and come right on home." She turned decisively and went into her bedroom.

No point arguing, Sam thought. There's not apt to be money for two tickets. Spending this much means she won't get something else she needs. And I stew about dumb things like swimming and baseball after school.

Questions crowded together in his mind, and he tried to shove them away as he always did. She feels bad enough, he told himself, without bringing up all my aches and pains. Sam Many Troubles, he reminded himself, I'll feel better tomorrow after I talk to Clete. I'll tell him what happened, but nobody else.

"The bus comes through at ten o'clock," she called out. "There's a four-hour wait along the way to transfer, and I'll get there tomorrow afternoon. Funeral's the next day, but tomorrow's bus would be too late. I'll be back the day after, depending on schedules. While I'm gone, you eat your suppers up at the cafe where the bus stops."

Sam looked at the food on his plate and shoved it away. "Couple meals aren't much to get," he said, "I'll cook a can of hash or something."

"Can of hash! That's just what you'd have. No, you eat some good solid food. You need it, working all day."

Sam sighed. "I'll carry your suitcase to the cafe."

"Never mind. It's not far. You get your rest. Why don't you stop all that running while I'm gone? Makes no sense anyway when you work every day."

Sam didn't answer. He knew she fussed about his sleep because she was always tired herself. She never understood how running was better than sleeping or eating or anything. He never felt shut out when he was running.

"It's not late," he said, "let me carry the suitcase."

She glanced around as if there were something she had forgotten, a reason to delay. Then she folded a sweater over her arm, smoothly, precisely, because that took longer. "Yes, Sam," she agreed, "walk with me to the corner."

Twilight covered the town. Streetlights shone here and there among the low houses. Sam thought everything seemed settled for the evening but themselves. The pasteboard suitcase seemed bale-heavy in his hand.

Under the corner light, his mother hesitated again. "I'll take the first bus back. No reason to stay longer. It'll be finished proper."

They glanced away from each other awkwardly.

33

Then she touched his shoulder lightly. "You're growing tall," she said, almost to herself. "A tall young man."

She seized up the suitcase and walked off quickly along the dark road leading to the bus stop.

"Good-bye," Sam called. There was no sign that she heard.

When he stepped back inside their small house, a floorboard creaked underfoot and echoed in the empty room. The open bedroom door gaped as dark as the mouth of a cave, and he pulled it shut. He switched on a table lamp. Even so, a dull, hollow feeling remained.

Sam nibbled at the cold food left on his plate, but it tasted greasy. He cleared off the table and stacked the dishes. Do them tomorrow, he thought.

He switched on the radio to fill up the silence and drown his thoughts. His favorite station blared out country western music and invitations to order record collections and *huaraches* and plastic cameras and secret dog-whistles, while they last. The music grated and the commercials rattled dully, but the stillness remained.

Sam wound the clock and set the alarm. If I feel good in the morning, he told himself, I'll push the run farther. Not too much, just enough. 'Course if Bud comes by, he can't run that far, not starting out, so I'll have to rein in. I'll show him how to pace himself, coach him along. It might be okay at that, running with someone. Maybe we'd get to be friends. That'd be okay, too.

He glanced around the room and fought down a tightness in his throat. Stop it, he told himself. Stop kidding. Bud won't come. He wanted to . . . sound friendly. Not that I care. I don't care. Why should I? I'd have to rein in if he did come. Sam took a deep gulp of air and let it out long and slow. I wish I could run right now, he thought, run till I couldn't lift my feet.

Sam kicked off his shoes and unrolled an old quilt from the arm of the couch. Skip pajamas, he decided, it's a waste of time getting dressed every morning. He turned off the lights and flopped down, numb.

"I don't even remember his face," Sam whispered. "A man ought to leave more than a shadow. I ought to know more about him than that."

In all the house there was not a photograph to tell him how his father had looked. There was not a patched work shirt that could have held the outline of a thin figure. There was nothing. 1955257

I wonder if she burned it all, he thought suddenly, like in Clete's story. He's been the same as dead all this time, just gone like a puff of smoke.

Then Sam sat up slowly, as if listening. A tall young man, his mother had called him. What did she mean? Had he gone from being a boy into being a man? The idea scared him.

Clete said a vision gave you power, he remembered, for the rough spots. Boy . . . right now . . . right now is when I need it.

He groped for the table, switched on the light and

found a sheet of paper and a pencil. Carefully he wrote: *Lawrence McKee, father of Sam. Tall and skinny shadow.*

Put in the made-up parts, he thought: *Pilot, gold miner, cowboy, ocean explorer, traveler.* Put in the real, what I know of it: *He left us, he went away, he never came back.*

Sam stared at the sheet, until his eyes stung with tears. At last he wrote in shaky letters: *Why didn't you come back? I could have tagged after you.*

He carried it to the stove, struck a match and set fire to the paper. Flame burst along the edge, yellow, flaring, curling into ashes. When it hurt his hand, he dropped the paper into the sink and watched until the flame died.

In darkness he sank back onto his bed. The sour smell of burned paper hung in the air, and the wondering stayed in his mind.

4

Sam slept fitfully, troubled; dreaming and waking seemed the same. It was a relief when he saw the sky lighten to gray and knew night would soon be over. He dozed quietly awhile, then woke again before the alarm clock rang and sat up, restless and eager to run.

He pulled his leather running shoes from the closet and laced them. One good thing I got from my job, he thought as he admired the white shoes with their red racing stripes.

He rinsed his mouth with water, not swallowing but wetting it against the time it would be desperately dry.

Outside, the air was cool. Sam jogged to loosen up. The first steps jarred, as he knew they would. His muscles were tight, sleepy. It takes a few steps, he thought, takes my legs a while to wake up. His back tensed, and he forced himself to exhale, exhale, until it relaxed.

Slow breath, slow breath, he coached himself, now exhale. Blow to exhale, more, more. In and in, out and out. Make it slow and natural. Not to think too much about it. If I run easy, I can push farther today. Every run I'm stronger.

Again and again his back muscles tensed, but he eased them. Loose and relaxed, his body would settle into the rhythm of the run. Tightened up, it fought and hurt, and breath came in stabbing gusts.

He stopped jogging at the corner where a narrow gravel road turned south to the reservoir, the dam. The road was fairly flat until it dipped down toward the water. Sam raised his shoulders and dropped them three times quickly, flexing and loosening those muscles. He felt good, full of power. No resting at the tree today, he told himself.

For the first hundred yards of the gravel road, he

jogged; then he lengthened his stride, slowly, easily. He imagined himself moving in slow motion with long, rolling strides, stretching his legs until his whole body caught the rhythm.

The pace was easy at the beginning, no more tiring than a good walk. It's like flying to move this way, Sam thought. I feel so welcome here. I know every lump on the road and how my footbeat sounds. I can smell the sage in the air.

Sometimes as he ran, his mind played tricks on him, whispering, am I halfway there? And that upset the rhythm of the run and made Sam awkward, aware of himself. He would overwork his legs, pull his arms high and tight, gulp air through his mouth.

When this happened, when his muscles screamed "Stop," Sam refused to give in. He shortened his stride, straightened his back, swung his arms in butterfly circles to unkink the shoulders. He slowed his breathing, pushed the air from his lungs, drew it in again in a long rising wave and pressed it out again.

Better, he thought, feels better. Easy stride. It's coming back. Feels good. Feels strong.

Having soothed his body back into the tempo of the run, he looked at the water of the dam ahead, glass-smooth in the still morning, a deeper blue than the sky. There were bullheads in the dam. Sam fished for them on summer evenings. He hated the look of them. He didn't even like taking them off the hook, but he did it, and his mother cooked them so they tasted better than anything.

He wondered where she was at that moment. Riding? Waiting? Must have been a long night for her, he thought. Hope she won't worry about me. His own empty feeling was less here on the road. He felt loose and free. This is how it feels, he thought, with the circle of the world around you. I wonder, would a vision quest make you feel this way? Like you had something of your own . . . something special.

The sun was high enough now so Sam felt it on his cheek. What a day it's going to be, he thought. I'll try it today. I'll push it farther. No stopping. Circle the big cottonwood and start back. Nonstop. See how far I can push.

Immediately his mind rebelled. Too far, it said, too tired. I'm always tired here, he answered himself, that's why I have to push farther. I won't quit.

He sighted on a clump of cone flowers. I'll run to those, he thought. And when he was close to them, he picked a gnarled fence post. I'll run that far, he thought. And when he was abreast of it, he turned his eyes on the cottonwood ahead.

I'm going to do it, he told himself. This is the time to make my break. Exhale now, out and out. Easy in the back. In and in, out and out. Put some kick into it.

His head was held high, his back straight to keep his

stride full. His face, streaked with sweat, glowed with a half smile, and his eyes didn't waver from the tree. There was no one to see him. A meadowlark sang from a fence post and flew off in alarm.

He circled the tree, which stood at a Y in the road, beside a path to the fishing dock. His grin widened, but he kept the pace steady. He reached out with one hand as if to mark the tree where he often stopped. If anything, he ran stronger and freer, having passed this goal.

I'm around, he thought gleefully. Feels good. Feels so good I may run right through town and out the other side. Easy . . . easy . . . steady does it.

The town lay ahead now, still drowsing; his own house no larger than a toy. Without warning he thought of the emptiness waiting there. It flooded over him, shoving him off stride, trapping his breath like a stone in his throat. His joy in the run vanished as quickly as a birdsong. He almost stumbled, so heavy were his feet.

And then his glance caught the mountain shapes in the north, soft, hazy gray in the yellow morning light. Dream mountains, he thought with some of the heaviness melting away. There they are, waiting. Someday, Clete and I'll go on up there and have a look. I'd like to find that place with the whole world around me. Not me on the edge.

Sam moved steadily again, his mind caught up in imagining a far-off vision quest. I wonder, could a dream make it so you'd never feel empty or left out? That'd be something. Clete'd know. I'll ask Clete. Ask Clete. Ask Clete. His footsteps seemed to pound out the words.

Caught up in his thoughts, Sam heard nothing on the road behind him. When a horn blared almost at his elbow, he jumped aside, turned and stopped.

It was a pickup, painted FRESH EGGS AND PRODUCE on the side. The driver laughed and waved. He shouted something like "Hup, two, three!"

Sam managed a short wave. The pickup left a choking swirl of blue dust in the air. Sam leaned forward, arms braced against his knees, and struggled to ease his breath. He felt his heart pounding, heard the pumping in his ears.

Broke my stride, he thought in disgust. Why'd that man have to honk at me? Couldn't he just drive on past?

Slowly Sam straightened and looked back at the reservoir. Halfway home. Tired as he was, a wide grin beamed across his face. All the way out and halfway back. I didn't even feel it, he thought, not till I had to stop. I was going good. I really did it.

5

Sam pulled on clean work pants and the old, tooled western boots he liked to wear on sale day. After his running shoes, the boots pinched his toes, but a hobble was a small price for a cowboy. He was glad to pull the door shut behind him and leave the lonely house.

At the stockyard, cattle trucks were backed against unloading chutes. Ranchers milled and mingled, jawed, laughed, swore, argued and examined their neighbors' beef before the sale. The corrals rang with bawls and baahs. In the dusty parking lot, little kids played tag, darting and shrieking among the cars. Their mothers were uptown shopping and visiting.

Best day of the week, Sam thought, sale day. And today the work would keep his mind off the heaviness that dogged him.

Mr. Weed motioned to him through the open office window. "You seen Clete?"

"I just got here," Sam said uncertainly. Was something wrong? "He must be around."

"He picked a poor day to sleep late," said Mr. Weed in a frazzled manner. He ran his fingers over what hair he had. "We got in enough livestock to keep us here selling till midnight, plus a shipment of hay that needs unloading. If Clete's not here, get Lester to help you and throw off those bales. And then see to the horses. . . ."

Another problem caused Mr. Weed to rake his thinning hair again. "That pinhead Lester . . . this morning he hit a horse so hard it's limping. How are we supposed to sell a horse like that? The owner is madder than a skinned weasel and I don't blame him. You check on the horses later. I don't want Lester near 'em."

Sam dodged through the parking lot and climbed the corral fence, looking for Clete. He's bound to be here, Sam told himself, after the way he kidded me about sleeping late.

Livestock jostled through the narrow aisles connecting the maze of pens, pushing and thumping against the wooden fences, eyes rolling in bewilderment. Sam hated seeing them prodded and hit to herd them along. That Lester, he thought, would enjoy it. Where could Clete be?

Not finding him, Sam called to the beefy, sullen-faced man who worked on sale day. "Hey, Lester! Help me unload those bales." He pointed at the flatbed truck parked behind the pens.

Lester shambled over to the fence and gaped at the truck. "All them bales?"

"Yeah, Mr. Weed says we gotta throw those off quick and get back to the livestock."

"Why don't Clete unload 'em?"

"He's . . . ah . . . busy, Lester. Come on."

Sam ran up a ramp at the rear of the truck and climbed onto the bales. "Better not be any snakes here waiting to surprise me," he muttered, shoving his hands into his gray work gloves. He looked again for the familiar, wiry shape of Clete, for the speckled hat.

"I need a hook," said Lester, eyeing the job as he ambled up.

"You don't," said Sam, "let's get this done!"

"Get my hook," Lester insisted. "Don't favor this work. I'm better with the livestock. . . ." He trailed away after the tool.

Sam glared after him. He bent to the nearest bale, grabbed the binding wire and pulled. It moved six inches. Sam hauled at it again, dragged it toward the ramp and let it slide to the ground.

Big bales like last night, he thought. Took both Clete and me to heft them. Now I'm carryin' the cow and Lester's bringing up the tail. Sam remembered how Clete sat to catch his breath, the deep lines alongside his mouth, the way he struggled up onto his feet. How many bales had Clete hauled alone and bone-tired?

Sam yanked another bale to the ramp and pushed it down. He tackled it as if making up for something. By the time Lester returned, a dozen bales lay at the bottom of the ramp. Sam wiped a rough glove over his forehead and said, "About time you got back."

"You could of waited. Who you trying to impress?"

"I'm getting the job done," Sam said.

"Well, ain't you a prize." Lester puffed up the ramp onto the truck.

They hauled in silence, swinging the bales between them. Sam's shoulders and back ached. I should have stayed last night, he repeated to himself, these are too heavy for one person, especially tired as Clete was. I should have stayed till the work was done.

Suddenly one bale slipped from Lester's hook so its full weight wrenched Sam's arms. He lurched forward and the bale pitched sideways, bouncing to the ground. The baling wire snapped and the hay spilled out.

"I almost fell off with that!" Sam yelled.

Lester only shrugged. His fleshy face was beaded with sweat. He held the hook stiffly at his side.

Sam stretched himself up as tall as he could. He was about half as big around as Lester. "Hang on to the next one," he said, glaring. "Now let's stack the ones on the ground so there's room for more."

Lester glowered. "You didn't say stacking. You said unloading."

"What'd you think . . . we'd leave them in a heap?" Be awful, Sam thought, if I had to work with Lester all the time. He'll blow up any minute and me with him. "It's all the same job . . . unloading and stacking."

"Then you stack, or let Clete do it. No kid orders me."

"Mr. Weed gave us the work."

"Like fun he did. He didn't tell me." Lester sat heavily on one of the bales. "I'm taking a rest."

"Okay, Lester. It's hot enough, that's sure. I'm going for a drink." Sam squatted at the side of the flatbed and jumped to the ground. He headed in the direction of the water fountain, but out of sight of the truck, he elbowed his way through the crowd, searching for Clete.

No one had seen the old man around the hog pens or the sheep pens or any of the cattle pens. Sam headed back to the truck with a worried frown.

Lester had disappeared, so Sam dragged the unloaded bales himself, lining them up by the corral fence. Then he slid others down, lugging and shoving until, finally, Lester returned. Neither of them spoke again. They piled up a loose, sloppy pyramid of bales. Lester didn't know how to stack properly, and Sam didn't push his luck trying to teach him.

When they finished, Lester marched off toward the lunch counter. Although Sam yearned for icy lemonade, he wasn't thirsty enough to chance sitting next to Lester. Instead Sam headed toward the horse pens, a job which usually pleased him. Today he found Lester hadn't watered them. Sam indignantly hauled a hose and opened it over the trough.

One horse, a black-and-white pinto, sniffed at the trough and eyed the boy. "Don't blame me," Sam said, "I didn't know you needed water." He felt guilty about it though. That's another thing I left for Clete, he thought, the watering.

The pinto nudged Sam's arm and he patted its strong neck. "What's the matter, boy? You scared of the commotion?"

Sam half expected Clete's head to pop into view over the fence, teasing. "Regular mother hen," Clete would say, "cluck, cluck, cluck . . ." Sam missed the old man.

Didn't seem like sale day without Clete. He ought to be telling a story to someone about now, Sam thought, smiling. Bet he's rehashed that cattle drive a hundred times. I could tell it myself.

Where is it Clete lives? North of town . . . that little house out by Bibbs' Dairy, Sam puzzled. Sure, he works at the dairy sometimes. Maybe that's where he is today. No, not on sale day. Could he be sick? It's almost noon; ought to be here if he's coming.

The pinto coaxed him for attention, and Sam stroked the long nose distractedly. "Can't talk today," he admitted. "I counted on seeing Clete."

Sam closed the pen gate and wandered into the sales barn to sit until Lester came out of the lunchroom. Lemonade would surely taste fine.

The air inside the barn was hot and stuffy and buzzing with flies. The semicircular bleachers around the sales ring were crowded near the windows, but Sam climbed to an empty section and plopped down, grateful for a rest.

In the ring below, six Hereford calves bunched together, skittish, swishing tails against the flies. The ring attendant flicked his whip to turn them and caught one calf across the eye. It stood bawling and blinking in confusion.

"Fine lot of young stock," said the auctioneer, seated at his high desk behind the ring. ". . . on range grass . . . good start for . . ."

The spiel droned around Sam's head, but he was not listening. Watching the calves reminded him of Clete's cattle plans. Seems like he ought to be around bragging about that ranch, Sam thought. Where is he today of all times?

"I got thirty," the auctioneer chanted, ". . . gimme ten, gimme ten, gimme ten . . . now half, now half, now half, now half. . . . Yeah!"

The buyers sat in clumps of three or four, talking, seeming to ignore the ring. But here and there a pencil wagged or a finger flagged, and with each sign, a ring attendant yelled "Yah . . . yeow . . ." and the bidding jumped.

"Now, five, five, five, five . . ."

"Yah!"

"And a quarter, and a quarter, and a quarter . . ."

"Yeow!"

Sam's head began throbbing in time to the chant. He pictured Clete again, slowly pushing himself up off the bales the evening before. I wonder if he could be sick, Sam fretted. It's a cinch he felt lousy last night, and yet he told me to go on home. Trying to make me feel better after what I said. I should have helped him finish.

Sam squirmed unhappily. Maybe Clete went someplace today. But why wouldn't he tell anyone? Should I go out to his house and see if he's there? How far is it to the dairy? A mile? Two? More like two.

Mr. Weed might give me a ride, except he's busy with the sale. Besides, if I ask him, he'll send me back to work and keep an eye on me. If I go, I better not tell anyone. Even if it's two miles, walking fast I can make it out and back in an hour. I'll be back before anyone knows I'm gone.

Sam climbed down from the bleachers, left by a side door and sprinted along the road. In the distance three tall, white silos marked the dairy farm near Clete's house.

6

Halfway to Clete's house, Sam felt foolish. He imagined the old man chuckling, "Think I'm so old I need checking up on? You upstart, I'll run both legs plumb off you."

Still it was strange Clete's not showing up for work, so Sam tracked along the gravel road. Ahead in the noon glare, the mountains stretched dark and solid. Sam smiled to himself. Maybe Clete had his fill of sleeping dreams and went off for a vision dream.

What would it be like, Clete? Would it turn you free the way running does? Maybe find your courage, find out what you were good for . . . or if you weren't good for much. Heavy gloom edged up on him again. I'll feel better once I find Clete and talk to him, Sam thought. I'm jumpy as a flea today.

The weathered frame house stood beside a fence line. Not so much as a thistle grew beside the house. Bare earth circled out to where the buffalo grass began. A footpath led through the ditch to the wooden-plank step at the door.

Sam knocked and waited. Behind the house he saw Clete's old black Chevy, two wheels balanced on blocks, a third flat. A two-lane track, thinly visible, angled across the field toward the dairy farm, another quarter mile away. He drew his attention back to the splintery door and knocked again.

Sam listened for any sound from inside and, hearing none, found a side window and cupped his hands around his eyes to peer inside. A catsup bottle stood on a table in front of the window. Opposite was a wood-burning cookstove. The back of the tiny room was shadowed, but a shape, perhaps a bed, lined the far wall. He couldn't be sure.

He returned to the door and pounded again. "Clete? Clete! It's me, Sam."

He tried the knob, found it unlocked and pushed the door open. "Clete?" Sam stepped inside where the air felt as hot and breathless as the barn had been. He quickly crossed the room.

The old man was lying on a sagging, steel-frame cot,

his eyes closed. Gray stubble flecked his cheeks and jaws and down onto his corded neck. His nose seemed more sharply arched than Sam remembered. Sam's hands trembled at his sides as he bent forward.

"Clete?" No response. Sam wasn't sure the old man was breathing or not.

"Clete?" Sam reached, faltered, reached again to touch the forehead. The skin felt cold and sticky. "Clete?" His voice cracked.

In response, one of Clete's arms twitched against the mattress. A sound struggled deep in his throat.

"It's me . . . Sam. Can you hear me?" In the silence his own voice rattled, hollow and far away. "Wake up. It's Sam."

After a moment, Clete's eyelids fluttered open. His dark eyes stared blindly at the ceiling, wavered and searched the space.

"It's me, Clete. Can you hear me? What happened?"

The dark eyes focused on Sam's face, warming slowly as he recognized the boy. His mouth opened, soundless until a moan escaped his throat.

Sam clenched his shaking hands into fists. Obviously Clete needed help. How long he had needed it, Sam did not want to guess.

"I'll get a doctor, Clete. I'll get a doctor right away." He knew almost without looking that there would be no telephone in the tiny house.

Clete's hand jerked again and again as if his body was

trying to speak. Wasn't there something Sam could do for him? A bucket of water and a dipper were on a stool. The old man couldn't drink, but Sam sprinkled drops onto his dry lips. A patched comforter was at the foot of the bed, and in spite of the stuffy room, Sam flung it open to cover Clete.

"I'll get help and be right back." He was almost shouting.

Clete's eyes were clearer. They followed Sam's movements as he opened the quilt. His mouth shaped thick and heavy sounds. Sam leaned close over the cot, listening, trying to lip-read.

"You . . ."—the old man's mouth worked grotesquely—"run . . . in . . ." Sam guessed wildly.

"Run? Yes, yes, I'll run," Sam said urgently. Clete didn't need to tell him that. "I'm going for help now."

Sam backed, frightened, toward the door. It felt wrong to leave the old man alone, but it had to be done. The dairy would have a telephone.

He sprinted along the dirt track. His boots weighed like wooden rockers attached to his legs and he wished for his soft running shoes. He raced toward the yellow farmhouse, thumped up the porch steps and pounded on the door.

No answer. He battered the door with the flat of his hand. The driveway was empty, but Sam saw the red, slatted tailgate of a truck parked near a low Quonset barn. He raced toward it, shouting "Hello? Anyone here?"

Squawks and flurries came from the barn. He pressed his face against the screened door. Dozens of white turkeys sputtered in protest and bustled away. No help there.

The folks must be in town, Sam thought in dismay. Maybe they're at the stockyard. Never occurred to me they'd be gone. What now? If the door's unlocked, I'll use the phone.

He bounded back to the house, high-jumped the porch steps and wrenched at the doorknob. It was locked. He beat again with his fist and hollered angrily, "Hey! Hey!"

Wasting time, he knew. Get back to the stockyard and tell Mr. Weed. But first, look in on Clete once more. Sam dashed back along the dusty path, gulping air until it swelled in his throat. He burst into the silent house.

"No one's home at the dairy." He crossed the room, breathless. "I have to run to the stockyard, I . . ." His voice caught, seeing Clete. The old wiry body was motionless. Not a finger twitched as sign that he heard. "I'll run," Sam repeated in a frightened tone, watching Clete's face. His lips seemed as gray as the stubble of beard. Sam pulled back.

He closed the door, scrambled across the path and broke into a run.

The pale clump that was the stockyard seemed hopelessly far. Already Sam's wind came hard; his arms rode high across his chest; his back was rigid. The pace was fast, too fast for the distance. He would never set such a pace on his morning run and his body knew it.

Slow up, Sam told himself, slow up and make it. It's too fast. I can't get my wind. Have to slow it.

Still he went on in choppy, windmill strides, strangling for breath, straining, wearing himself down. Slower, he pleaded, get a pace. Slow down.

There was no sense of himself in this run, no feeling of the world around him. There was only a pressure, an unseen wheel bearing down on him, pushing him painfully along the road.

In the soft, uneven gravel, his bootheels sank and twisted, tipping him off-balance, knotting the muscles of his calves. One slip pitched him forward and he threw out his arms to stop the fall. He stayed there on hands and knees, dragging air into his lungs, shaking his head to clear the dizziness.

Then he hauled himself onto his feet, though his legs shook and his side ached. The outline of the stockyard was clear now, yet a mile away. He forced his legs back into a run, jerky because the muscles hurt, and worked to steady his breathing. Huff out the old air, he thought automatically. Out and out. Still his lungs felt on fire.

For a moment Sam ran in terror of collapsing, crumpling into the ditch. The grasses waved, soft and welcoming. Not yet, he begged himself, I don't quit yet. Run. Run to that fence post. Run that far.

Groggy, Sam rounded the corner and pushed toward the stockyard. He heard the commotion and smelled the pens. Couldn't they see him coming? Why didn't someone see him? He pounded his feet along the road, clawing the air with his hands for breath. Get to Mr. Weed, he thought, get help.

Sam plunged through the parking lot toward the office and stopped stiff-armed against the door. He grabbed blindly for the handle until the door opened from inside.

"Sam! What's wrong?"

His chest heaved with the effort to speak. He recognized Mr. Weed's voice, but as dizzy as he was and with his head pounding, he could not make a sound.

"Sit down here."

Sam dropped his head forward onto his hands and choked out, "A doctor . . . for Clete . . ."

"For Clete? I don't . . . Have you been out to Clete's?"

Sam sucked in air, lifting his head urgently. "He's laid out . . . on his cot . . . can't move."

Mr. Weed swore and grabbed for the telephone. Sam heard him dial and speak to the doctor. "Yeah . . . that little house on this side of Gus Bibbs' dairy. I'll get up there myself and meet you. Sam says the old guy wasn't moving."

Sam's muscles quivered, and his face burned. Is this really happening? he thought.

"You okay?" Mr. Weed asked as he hung up the phone.

"I'll go with you," Sam said.

Mr. Weed frowned. "No need to, Sam. Why don't you go on and get yourself something cold to drink."

Sam struggled to his feet. "I have to go back," he said. He remembered Clete's face with a shudder, but he had to return. He had to know how Clete was. His legs swung like stilts as he followed Mr. Weed to the car.

"What do you think it is?" Sam asked in a dull voice. The car steamed out of the parking lot.

"Lord knows," said Mr. Weed. "Clete's getting along in years; it could be most anything. Did he look all right to you yesterday?"

"He seemed tired, I guess," Sam said slowly. Images of Clete, limp and asleep in the afternoon heat, Clete boosting himself up from the bales of hay, haunted him.

"Even so," Sam's voice shook, "he sent me home and finished up himself. Maybe if I'd stayed . . ."

"Don't think that way," Mr. Weed said quickly, shaking his head. "It's nothing to do with this. Why, he may just have some summer virus that made him feverish . . . too weak to move."

"His head wasn't feverish," Sam said quietly. "It was awful cold."

"Well, I don't know," Mr. Weed said. "We'll have to hear what the doc says."

56

They rode in silence after that. Mr. Weed parked the car on the shoulder of the road and hurried toward the house. Sam followed, dreading to see again Clete's face and his worn figure under the quilt.

By the time he reached the door, Mr. Weed had stepped back outside and met him. "Better wait in the car, Sam."

Sam saw his grim expression without wanting to understand. "But can't I see him?"

"There's no point. Clete is dead."

Sam reeled as though he'd been hit. "But I saw him. He talked to me."

"I'm afraid that's the last time he'll talk to any of us." Mr. Weed put an arm around Sam's shoulders and steered him away from the door.

Sam felt numb. Everything seemed to break and scatter around him. All he remembered was Clete's stubbled face.

His knees folded and Sam sank down in the grassy ditch. Tears stung his eyes and he didn't want Mr. Weed to see. His thoughts tangled together. If I'd stayed last night . . . when Clete was bone-tired . . . if I'd come out sooner . . . too much gone wrong at once . . . last night . . . now this. Sam doubled up, pains shooting through his stomach.

When the doctor's car pulled up, he and Mr. Weed spoke in low tones. Sam knew they went into the house. In a few moments Mr. Weed returned and headed for his car.

He hesitated beside the boy. "I'm sure sorry," he said. "Clete was partial to you. He surely was. You did your best by him, Sam."

Sam choked down a sob. He could not look up. His best? Running was his best and it had failed him.

"I'm going back to the office to make a phone call. You may as well ride back. Nothing to be done here." He waited, then stepped toward his car. "Coming?"

Sam barely shook his head.

"No? Well . . . a man needs time to think, chew things over . . . so long as it doesn't start eating on you. Go home today if you want . . . we'll get along."

Sam heard the heavy car door slam and the gravel clatter as Mr. Weed drove away. A phone call, he realized with another twist in his stomach, meant someone would come for Clete. Got to get away from here before that, he thought.

Sam pushed himself up onto his feet. He couldn't face his own empty house. It would feel as empty as Clete's. The stockyard? To Lester and a crowd that wouldn't care about Clete? Where then?

"Where can I go?" he whispered. He was on the outside of the circle. Not even Clete to help him. I'm sorry, Clete, he wanted to shout, if I'd been faster . . . or sooner . . . or . . .

His chest hurt from the run, but not a good, satisfying ache. It burned like a branding iron. Without choosing, he began to jog, to free himself from the hurt.

He jolted stiffly along the road, and when he was breathless and hot and his eyes brimmed with tears, he stopped and looked up. What he saw, far ahead, misty and inviting, were the mountains. We won't ever go up there together, Clete, he thought. Any more than you'll have that ranch you dreamed about.

Sam wished he were there in the mountains, someplace high and cool where he could sit and chew things over, away from the pounding inside his head.

Find a vision, like Clete said. Why not? If it helped the old-time Indian boys have courage, why not him? Truly, he didn't believe it would happen that way, but he needed thinking time. He needed to ease the heaviness. Sam Many Troubles.

I'll call it my vision quest, he thought hopefully. Maybe I'll find a power after all, a spirit to help me. Besides, there's nowhere else to go.

7

Walking beside the highway Sam seemed all angles. His hands were shoved into his pockets so the elbows jutted out, his head and shoulders bowed forward. The cowboy boots gave a stiff-legged jolt to his step, unlike his loose running stride.

His thoughts moved stiffly, too. On my way, Clete. Hunting a vision. In the mountains where you said. Hunting a power to make me big enough, make me special. Hah. I'm sure special; no father, no friends, no Clete. I'm one of a kind already. Clete said there were dreams in the mountains. Clete's dead. How can it be?

A cattle truck passed Sam, then stopped with a screech of brakes. Sam ran to catch up and hauled himself up into the cab. At once he felt caught between the noise of the engine in front and the cattle bawling behind him and the blistering air blowing in through the side windows. At least it's a ride, he told himself.

"I'm headed north through the mountains," said the driver, a burly man set to handle a truck or anyone who argued with him. "Going far?"

"Same direction," Sam said. "I appreciate the ride. Hot out there."

"Glad for company," the driver shouted over the engine's roar. "Talking keeps me awake on a long haul." He grinned at Sam. "These cattle will quiet down. They complain starting out—makes them feel better. Just like people. I picked up this load at Weed's stockyard. Know the place?"

Sam barely nodded, but the driver went on. "Oh, I look hitchhikers over carefully first," he said. "Just the guys who need a ride . . . none of those barefoot free-loaders for me. I can pretty well tell the kooks." His eyes narrowed, thinking about them.

Sam watched the road. He didn't want to talk, certainly not to explain what he was doing. He hardly knew what he was doing when it came to that. But moving on made it easier. Motion seemed necessary to lighten this feeling inside him. He hadn't counted on a chatty driver.

"I said, where are you heading?"

Sam started guiltily. The question brought him back to the hot cab. "Oh . . . I . . . I . . ." he floundered. "My uncle lives up north. Ah . . . up around Vista." It was the first town he remembered and he turned his face quickly to hide the lie.

"That so? Pretty country. I lived around there. Used to hunt wild horses in the mountains. What's his name? Maybe I know him."

"I don't think so . . . he hasn't been there long." That's for sure, Sam thought.

"Try me," said the driver. "I know lots of people out that way. What's his name?"

Sam was trapped. He grabbed a handy name. "Gus. It's Gus . . . ah . . . Anderson." And don't ask me any more, he pleaded silently.

"Nope," said the driver. "You got me on that one. Don't know him." He shook his head. "Knew a Harvey Anderson once, but he moved. Does he ranch?"

Now Sam was stuck for a livelihood for his make-believe uncle. He couldn't make a joke of the whole thing either, not without being put out of the truck like a kook. "He's got a small place," Sam said slowly as he remembered something. "Not very big. He raises turkeys."

"Turkeys!" The driver lifted his eyebrows, as surprised as Sam was at this information. "Well, I'll be . . . a turkey ranch."

"Is it far now?" Sam changed the conversation, hoping his blown-up fib wouldn't backfire.

"Maybe I did hear about a fellow starting in to raise turkeys," said the driver, frowning. "Over by the Big Crow River? Or was it the Little Crow?"

Sam fidgeted. "I'm not too familiar. Might be one of those." Shouldn't have said turkeys, Sam thought, made him too curious. "Isn't Vista close to the mountains?"

"Sits smack in the foothills," the driver said. "I wonder where your uncle sells those turkeys. Does he truck them himself?"

"Those mountains look real close now. How far is it?" Sam tried to head off the conversation.

"You give your uncle my name, case he ever needs a trucker for those birds."

"Will another hour get us there? It's sure hot on the road." Sam kept trying.

"I got a small truck would haul, oh . . . let's see, how many crates . . ."

"People say it's the driest summer in years . . . fire weather, they say."

"Unless he hauls for himself, of course. Could have his own truck."

"A good rainstorm is what we need."

"Tell you what—there's a sales bill in the glove compartment with my name and phone number on it. You give it to your uncle."

Sam gave up on the weather and dug through the gritty maps and papers in the small compartment. "I got one," he said, shoving it into his shirt pocket.

"That's fine. You give him that, case he ever needs a hauler. I don't imagine he drives those turkeys overland, do you?" He laughed heartily and Sam mustered a weak grin.

"That'd be a sight, wouldn't it?" the driver went on. "Lot of wranglers riding herd . . . turkey-boys instead of cowboys." He guffawed and whacked the steering wheel in delight. "You going out to be a turkey-boy?"

Sam's mouth ached from trying to smile. "No. Just visiting."

"Yeah, I guess you would be. Say, you're traveling pretty light . . . come to think of it."

Sam shifted uneasily. "Ah . . . he's got a boy my age, so we swap clothes. No need to carry anything with me."

The driver pursed his mouth thoughtfully. "Your folks know you was going?"

"Oh, sure! Sale day is a good chance to catch a ride. Oh, it's all right."

"I hope so. I don't hold with kids taking off on their own."

"Oh, no. Neither do I."

"What's the name of that cousin of yours?"

"Gus."

"I thought that was your uncle."

"Uh, yes . . . he's Gus and my cousin's Gus, too." Sam struggled with the family history. "They're Big Gus and Little Gus."

"Yeah?" said the driver. "If Little Gus is your size, he's not so little."

"No," Sam said slowly, "but he used to be real little."

"Hmm," the driver said and was silent as they drove on. Finally he switched on the radio.

Sam turned back to the window with relief, seeing sandy ditches filled with yucca and prairie grass. The fields and pastures seemed terraced where the sand lay in blown ridges beneath the grass. Old tires ringed the telephone poles to keep the soil from drifting and dislodging the poles. Each hill crossed helped Sam put a distance between himself and what had happened. Miles passed. An hour passed.

Roads leading off the main highway were marked with high signboards: EMMETT RANCH, 5 MILES; X BAR L, 9 MILES; BLUEBELL RANCH, 17 MILES. Could have had your name on a sign, Clete, the boy thought suddenly. Maybe that cottonwood and stream are right around here . . . in sight of the dream mountains. You'd like it, Clete.

A memory of the old man lying so still lashed at Sam. The land blurred behind sudden tears. Don't cry, he warned himself, don't cry. You can't. You're stuck with that stupid Gus Anderson story. Make the best of it.

"Coming into Vista soon," said the driver. "Any special place you want off? I usually stop at the Wheel Inn Cafe myself."

Sam coughed to clear his throat before he could say "That's fine." He braced himself as the truck jolted into a lower gear as the road began to climb.

"Can you call your uncle?"

"Oh, I expect he's waiting around the post office," Sam said quickly. "I'll walk on. I'm much obliged for the ride."

"Well, if you think he'll be there, that's okay then. I'm coming through on Wednesday if you want a ride back."

"I guess my uncle'll drive me home."

"Him and Little Gus, huh?"

"Probably," Sam muttered. The driver chuckled.

Sam read the name VISTA painted across the water tower. The highway ran straight through town toward the peaks beyond. Sam needed to find a back road into the mountains to avoid meeting the trucker again on the main highway.

"Buy you some pop?" the driver asked as they stopped.

Sam jumped down from the cab. "No, thanks. I better see if my uncle's waiting."

"I sure hope he is. The post office is that way." The

driver waved in the opposite direction from the way Sam was moving. Sam nodded and tried to saunter away as if he knew it all along.

Wonder how long it'll be, he thought, before that trucker asks a waitress about Gus Anderson, the big turkey rancher. He turned onto a side street and followed it out of town.

There the gravel road paralleled a line of red buttes, standing like sentinels before the mountains. Made it this far, he thought, it can't be much farther. The late afternoon sun burned his face, and he wiped his forehead on his sleeve. What I wouldn't give for a piece of Mina's pie or a nap in the shade like Clete. No, not like Clete, not anymore.

He jumped aside as a car passed him, leaving a tunnel of dust. It skidded around a corner ahead and sped on until it disappeared between the buttes. There's a road going into the mountains, Sam realized. I can follow that one.

Sam was hot and dry, thirsty enough to forget he was also hungry. The fields offered no shade. To the east were ranch buildings, but out of his way. If he found a place near the road, he would ask for a drink.

Although the buttes seemed close, he hiked almost an hour to reach them. Along the way he paused to touch the fluttering white petals of a wild poppy, rising fresh from a cracked, parched ditch. He didn't remember ever seeing such a flower. Even the sage of these fields was a type new to him, tall silver-green spires the size of seedling trees. He felt he was entering a new country.

The road curved up onto a small plateau where a light breeze ruffled his hair, and Sam faced into it gratefully. Against the lowering sun one fence post looked thicker than the others, and he crossed the road toward it, then jerked back with a gasp.

A coyote hung head-down, hind foot nailed to the top of the post. One sightless, glassy eye glinted through the weeds at Sam. Danger, it seemed to whisper. The image of Clete's dark sunken eyes rushed over Sam like a half-forgotten nightmare. He stumbled away, glancing over his shoulder at the dead animal.

The road jogged briefly right and then left, as though it had been built from opposite ends without meeting at the center. Sam followed it, distracted and queasy from seeing the coyote. He almost missed a familiar shape standing near the jog. Then he shouted, "A windmill!"

He ran to the barbwire fence and, after checking hastily for livestock, squeezed through. A blue enamel cup hung like an invitation on the pump.

A drainpipe connected the pump to a cattle trough nearby. Sam unwired the pipe and carefully loosened the brake on the windmill. The propellers swung to the breeze, revolving slowly. Water dribbled, then gushed, from the pump.

Sam gulped a cupful without stopping. Best I ever tasted, he thought, and he drained a second cupful. Then he caught water in his hands and doused his face again and again. Finally he held his head under the stream of water and let it gush over his hair and into his ears and down his neck. Only when a puddle grew beneath the spout did he brake the whirling propeller and replace the pipe.

A breeze dried and cooled him as he went on. The road wound between the red shale buttes. Behind them low, barren hills showed strips of color: red and pink and tan. Scrub junipers dotted the slopes. I could use a rest, Sam thought. Might be cool under those trees.

The slope was steeper than he expected. His feet slipped in the loose, dry soil. When he tripped and caught himself, the earth was warm under his hands. His face streaked with sweat as he climbed.

On the crest of the hill was a juniper no taller than his chin. The trunk was the size of a fence post, gnarled and bent over itself. Branches splayed out and down, touching the ground like a bristly, green tent. There was a small opening on one side where the branches parted.

Sam crawled inside. Chips of bark covered the ground, and the shade was juniper scented. He pinched loose a needle and crushed the fragrance against his skin.

He ached from the soles of his feet to the back of his neck, too tired to feel anything else. Not sadness, not emptiness. He stretched out and almost at once fell asleep.

When he woke, a soft golden light promised sunset, and he moved out from his shelter to watch. He sat cross-legged, feeling the cool air as it rose from the long shadows of the valley below. The sunset flamed low with no clouds to play the colors across the sky. Idly Sam plucked a leaf of sage and bit into it. The bitter flavor exploded in his mouth. He retched and spat it out, shuddering, choking. The nausea brought loneliness. He wished he could close his eyes and awaken on his own sofa, even in the too-empty house. Whatever can I find here? he thought dismally.

He noticed a movement on the next ridge, a column of dust spinning along the top. Then a mare and colt loped into view over the crest. Two more mares and another colt followed, all silhouetted against the glowing sky. The colts tucked their heads against their mothers. The mares listened and waited.

Another horse appeared on the hilltop, nosing the air, turning its head from side to side. This must be a wild herd, Sam realized in amazement. That last is the stallion. Look at him. His tail's so long it rakes the ground.

Sam hunched low, wishing he were behind his juniper tent. The horses stayed alert for sounds behind them. They had not sighted Sam, and the wind, blowing toward him, carried his scent away. Stealthily he flattened against the ground.

The mares began browsing, edging downhill. The stallion waited, listening and wary. He dipped his head to the grass and raised it again to test the air. Then, searchingly, his gaze swung in Sam's direction.

The boy froze, scarcely breathing or blinking. The

horse waited, statue still. As though on command, the mares also stopped grazing and looked toward Sam.

It was impossible to know how the horses sensed him, but they knew. The mares and colts drifted together, slowly at first, picking their way over the rough ground. They traveled the short valley and trotted up the slope, putting distance between themselves and Sam.

As they topped the hill, the stallion followed on the run. He paused on the ridge to pivot, testing the four directions, then disappeared after the mares.

Sam pushed himself up eagerly. I could hike to the next ridge, he thought, but the horses would probably be gone. If I keep my eyes open, maybe I'll find them again. The sight of the horses made the hillside less lonely. Keep my eyes open, he repeated.

His juniper tent felt familiar when he crawled back inside. In the growing darkness, he sensed the night creatures giving the juniper a wide berth. He glimpsed a small shadow scudding from one clump of sage to another.

He heard the peppery yaps of the prairie dogs gossiping in the summer evening, and the frantic ruffling of a bird frightened into flight, the rhythmic beating as it gained height.

Sam tugged off his boots, and instantly a mosquito hovered over their warmth. He curled on his side, pillowing his head on an arm.

Images of his home and a half-remembered shadow

and of Clete crowded into his mind. He was too exhausted to cry. What good did going away do? he wondered. Might as well go on back. Nothing will ever change. Never find any power here. Not me.

But then he pictured the white poppy growing in the crusty soil. And he thought of the horses running free. I'd like to see them again, he told himself. No reason to go home yet. Haven't gone far into the mountains yet. And slowly he eased into sleep.

Once in the night he woke, frightened, lost. He stretched up one hand and touched the prickly juniper needles where moonlight made them glisten. He peered out at the clay hills, fragile in this light, almost a moonscape.

"Dream country," he whispered, lying back against the ground. He watched the few stars visible through the branches. Feels like a swing, he thought drowsily, must be the earth moving.

8

Gray sky showed between the branches. There was a soft ripping beyond the juniper which made Sam lie silent, wondering about it, feeling a cramp in one leg but not wanting to move and risk a noise.

Finally, a low snuffle let him know there was a horse on the hill beside him. Sam rolled onto his hands and knees. Each needle snap seemed to thunder in his ears. Outside, the browsing continued, with a low snort from time to time. If he surprised a wild horse, would it attack?

Timidly he poked his head through the opening. It was a single horse, a mare, black with three white stockings. She snorted, startled, and sidled away. Sam didn't remember her from the herd he had seen, and he wondered if she was wild.

The horse stopped and peered at Sam, more indignant than frightened.

"Did I scare you?" Sam asked, speaking softly. Inch by inch he crawled from under the tree. The mare watched cautiously.

"Don't look so suspicious," he said. "Think I'm going to steal your breakfast?" He wished he hadn't mentioned breakfast.

Sam pulled on his boots. The mare sidestepped off when he stood up. "Easy now," he said. "You all alone here? Will you let me come closer?"

He kept his voice low, the way he talked to animals at the stockyard, and took four slow steps while the horse regarded him.

"Now, girl. Be friends. Don't be afraid. A few more steps."

Warily she dipped her head and wheeled away.

"Phooey," Sam muttered. The mare slowed and turned to watch him again. "I'm not chasing you up and down these hills," he said. "Go eat your breakfast. You're lucky you have one."

But since he didn't know where else to go, Sam followed the horse's lead. She sauntered on, cocking her head to keep him in sight.

The horse led the boy across the valley to the next slope with a constant space between them. Close enough for Sam to talk to her but never reach her, even when he tried slyly to close the distance.

Sam was hungry and the prospect of no food made it worse. The clink of change in his pocket, enough for breakfast in town, made him look back. All he saw was the ridge from which he had come.

It won't be much of a vision quest, he told himself, if I'm always going into town to eat. The mare continued ahead, head bobbing as she went. Just under the crest of a hill, she stopped, sniffed the air and whirled away. She rounded the slope and disappeared. Sam felt deserted. He scrambled to the top, hoping to see her.

Below was a steep canyon, blue shadowed, with the slate-colored reflection of a creek meandering through it. Moving toward the water was a horse, not the black mare but a buckskin. Sam hoped the horse would not see him against the bright, rising sun at his back. Slowly he eased behind a juniper cover.

The buckskin, a stallion, pretended to drink as he

studied the surroundings. Then he turned toward a shadowy cut, and his low whinny carried on the air.

Faint clops sounded as two mares and a colt came from the cut. A moment later another mare appeared. They filed cautiously toward the creek. The stallion dipped his head and drank deeply. When the mares reached the water, he moved to higher ground, on guard again.

Sam held his breath as the buckskin came closer, grazing. Not an imaginary wild horse, sleek and beautiful, but a real one with a wide rump and thick neck. In the sunlight, old scars showed on his shaggy hide. Across his chest was a single line, barbwire thin. Look at that old boy, Sam thought, carries those marks like battle ribbons.

He had never seen such a buckskin. Its legs were banded behind the shanks, almost zebra striped. The stallion tore quietly at the grassy clumps on the hillside. Below, the mares and colt watered and browsed.

Sam squinted to find unusual markings on the mares, but they were too deep in the shadows. He froze when the stallion snorted a low command. Was he discovered?

There was no further alarm. The horses moved leisurely away, dipping their heads to the grass as they went. The stallion grazed until the mares reached the far bend, then he trotted close enough to maintain his watch. After a last nibble of grass, he followed them.

Only then did a noise cause Sam to turn his head toward a nearby juniper.

A woman, dressed in dungarees and a denim jacket,

crawled out from under a tree, dragging a folded umbrella and knapsack. She nodded in his direction as she stood up and headed toward him.

"Good thing the sun's at our back," she called. "Thought you'd spook the whole bunch, shambling over the top the way you did."

She lowered her sack to the ground and sat down beside Sam. Her eyes seemed the same blue as the denim and just as creased about the edges. Her hair, a mixture of gray and tan, was short and uneven, as though she cut it herself on various days.

"Name's Mrs. Mellette," she said, "though most folks call me Mrs. Em, after Emma. Care for some coffee?"

Sam was too surprised to know what to say.

Without waiting, she pulled a thermos from her bag, poured a capful and handed it to Sam. "I have only this one cup, but it won't hurt you. How do you happen to be here? I don't usually have company unless the B.L.M. has a man out inspecting . . . or snooping . . . depending on how you look at it."

"B.L.M.?"

"Bureau of Land Management. A government operation."

Sam drank the warm coffee eagerly. It slid down, warming him inside as the sun warmed his shoulders.

"I didn't know there'd be horses here," he said, collecting his thoughts. "I was following after an old mare and she suddenly took off. I stumbled onto this bunch."

"A single mare? Three stockings?" Mrs. Em smiled

and nodded. "That's Belle. At least, that's my name for her. She's a loner, probably too old for a harem. What a character . . . curious about people . . . she hangs around to watch me when I'm out here."

"She let me follow her," Sam said, "but only so close."

"Led you right to me, did she? That's as good as an introduction. What's your name, son?"

"Sam." He wondered if she was going to ask a lot of questions.

She waited and then went on. "A nice name . . . Sam. Odd, Belle didn't show herself to me."

"She went off that way." Sam jerked his thumb toward the right.

"Heat's coming on. She'll find some shady draw for the afternoon. By evening she'll be around again."

Sam finished the coffee and felt better. "I saw horses last night. In the valley back there. A stallion, three mares and two colts."

Mrs. Em nodded. "Old broomtail stallion? I know that band, too. Come out here often enough and you get to recognize the different harems. He's an old one . . . come through some hard times from the looks of him. Lately there's a bunch of young stallions traveling around here, looking for their own harems. Sooner or later one of them is bound to challenge that broomtail. There'll be skin flying that day."

"You mean they'll fight?"

"Will they ever! Oh, sometimes they don't challenge

outright, they try to steal away a mare or two. But the old boy won't stand still for that, so either way they'll have it out."

"Ever see a stallion fight?"

"Once. And that was enough. Bellowing, biting and kicking like you never saw."

"Sounds cruel," said Sam.

"Guess it's natural for them. The young mustangs have to grab what they want. Tough survival out here. Hardly anything to eat in the winter, not much more in the summer. Last winter the B.L.M. dropped a planeload of hay along the ridge. That hay and the horses' own grit and maybe a miracle got them through."

Sam considered the horses with excitement and sadness. The buckskin running free was one thing, but pushing through snowdrifts hunting food was something else. And how would a colt stand a winter like that?

"Must be hard on the loners, like Belle," he said.

"Yes, yes. Not just the winters but being alone makes them an easy target . . . good dog-food candidates."

"Dog food?"

Mrs. Em nodded. "It's not legal, not since these wild herds are protected by the government, but there's still a fellow here and there likes to sneak into the hills and see if he can get something free."

"But that's stealing."

"Some people figure stealing is taking what belongs to someone else," said Mrs. Em. "Taking a horse that's free, they aren't so shy about that. And some ranchers think, who's to know if they come up here and make a little canyon corral and trap a horse and truck him back down to the home range? They go so far's to say they're doing the horse a favor, giving him feed and range.

"Most wild horses, though, don't mix well with domestic ones. They're small and tough, no real beauties, but they have staying power; they're rugged."

"What finally happens to them?" asked Sam.

"A rancher'll try to breed them to get some of that stamina in a horse of his own that he can train and handle. Sometimes they try to break a wild horse to ride, and not many can do that these days. Usually they end up breaking their what-have-you and get mad at the horse when it's their own fool fault."

She took a deep breath. "About that time they decide the horse isn't worth the trouble and sell it. Dog food, like I said. Some fellows skip the in-between steps and sell it right off. The profit's the thing."

Mrs. Em laughed. "Course it also happens the other way around. The wild stock does a little rustling. Some young stallion after a harem will go down to a ranch herd and entice a mare away, or get himself roped and caught and then break loose with two or three of the rancher's mares. Could be Belle was tame once, being so uncommonly sociable for a wild horse."

Abruptly she changed the subject. "You didn't say how you came to be here, how you happened to see the horses last night. . . . If you don't mind my asking."

Sam weighed his answer. Uncle Gus was too chancy. He looked toward the mountains with an idea. "I heard there were tipi rings around here. I came to see them."

"Tipi rings?" Mrs. Em echoed. "You're some miles off course. What'd you want to see them for?"

"Oh, I . . . thought they sounded interesting. . . ." He fumbled for an answer. "And historical. Kind of a history lesson."

"So . . . you're a student of history," she said slowly. "Let's hope it's better than your geography." She got up and brushed off her jeans. "Come on." She gathered up her knapsack and umbrella. "I could use a bite of breakfast, and I never knew a boy who wasn't hungry." She tramped along the crest of the hill. "It's a mile or so to my place."

Sam didn't know what to do but follow. His stomach was pinched for food. A grasshopper whirred up from a yucca, and Sam jumped.

Mrs. Em laughed. "They startle me, too. I always figure a six-foot rattler comes with that whirr. Never has, but I still jump."

"Did you come up just to watch the horses?"

"Partly. They're down to water early morning and twilight. Rest of the day they're higher in the mountains where it's cooler and the grazing's better. Grazing's not good anywhere right now. We sure need rain. It's so dry a cricket rubbing his legs together could spark a fire.

"I suppose we'll have a regular deluge one of these days," she said, shaking her head. "But since you asked . . . besides wanting to see the horses, I hunt for fossils. Last summer I found a perfect fish skeleton imprinted on a piece of shale."

"A fish skeleton? Up here in the mountains?"

"Think of your history now," said Mrs. Em, smiling. "These hills were part of the seabed once. Fact is, I find more fossils of the sea than of early animals, dinosaurs and such. Course the sea fossils are easy to recognize. I wouldn't know a dinosaur print if I tripped on it. A local fellow came across one, claimed it was the footprint of a saber-toothed tiger. Anyway, the university came out, dug it up and whisked it away before anyone knew what was happening."

Sam hurried to keep up with Mrs. Em, who wasn't even puffing. She slipped and skidded down an incline, caught her balance and went on talking with hardly a pause.

"Imagine all this as a sea," she said with a sweep of her arm, "where life began. That's what I told my children. We'd come out walking and I'd point out plants and rocks. They weren't so keen on the information, but they liked the outings. Never had one show an interest in the tipi rings, but I guess that comes of living so close to them."

It was a subject to make Sam squirm. He changed it. "How many children do you have?"

"Oh, hundreds," she said. "Over the years, I've had hundreds."

9

She's kidding me, Sam decided. No one has hundreds of children.

"Do you live on a ranch?" he asked. "With lots of livestock?"

Mrs. Em threw back her head and laughed. "Not exactly. I have a one-room house, a weedy garden . . . and no livestock, unless you count the wild horses."

A small house so far in the country? Sam thought it strange, but the lure of breakfast carried him along.

"I do have one piece of livestock," she added. "It's a baby I found. I keep it hidden because my neighbor wants to shoot it."

Sam stumbled. What kind of thing was that to say? His steps slowed. Maybe he ought to say good-bye and set off. They reached the crest of a hill.

"There it is," she said, pointing down the slope. "My 'ranch' as you call it."

Sam squinted. Gradually the shape became clear to him. "It's a schoolhouse!"

"Course it's a schoolhouse," said Mrs. Em. "I thought

the cat had your tongue. Come on. There's lemonade in the refrigerator."

She led the way, dodging between the clumps of prickly pear on the hillside. Sam followed, picking his way more slowly. He saw a gravel road beyond the school yard. Automobile tracks led to a small, gray shack in a corner of the yard.

"Enough children around here to fill up a school?" he asked.

"No," she said almost sadly. "There are children, but they're not mine anymore. They're bused to school in town. Even the little ones who ought to be playing out-doors after school, they travel for hours."

Sam grinned in relief. "That's what you meant by having hundreds of children."

Mrs. Em chuckled. "Yes. It's a conceit of mine, that and thinking they'd be better off here. Country schools are closed now. Progress, they say. Puts me out to pasture."

They reached the wooden gate in front of the house. "The school board promised me I could live here," she explained. "They about had to, every one of them had been to school to me. Abe Andrews wants me to move to town. He's got his eyes on this place. Wants to board it up for a granary."

In the yard a rusty merry-go-round hung lopsided. Heavy chain links clanked in a swing stand, but only the packed footpaths marked where the swings had been.

Sam followed Mrs. Em up three wooden steps and into

an entry room. There was one tiny window high on a wall, like a sky-blue painting. Under it a row of coat hooks held a woman's coat, a straw hat and a pink scarf. A shotgun leaned against an old metal trunk in the corner.

"Leave the door open for air," she said.

Sam pushed it back against the wall, where he noticed ladder rungs nailed between the bare studs. They led to a trapdoor in the ceiling. It must go up to the bell tower, he decided.

There were no desks in the sunny main room, but Sam saw the old marks of floor bolts in rows between the tall side windows. Now the room held a wooden table and three chairs; an overstuffed sofa, covered with a red-and-blue Indian blanket; and a honey-colored oak desk. A glassed-in case had shelves of books and one shelf filled with strange rocks and a fish fossil.

Mrs. Em pulled a pitcher from the small refrigerator in her corner kitchen and poured two glassfuls. She cut two wide slices of chocolate cake and motioned Sam to a chair.

"This wouldn't win a 'good breakfast' award," she said, "but after that hike we deserve a treat."

Sam, hungry, bit off a huge piece of cake before he remembered the vision quest. He swallowed hard and decided Clete would approve of eating breakfast.

"I'm always cheered up when I see the horses," said Mrs. Em. "They're so scruffy and elegant and free, for all their hard life. By the way, how do you like my picture window?" She waved toward the far end of the room.

A pastel landscape of the mountains covered an old blackboard, running the width of the wall. Oversized wild flowers of all colors were painted along the bottom. At one side a slim vertical strip of blackboard had been left bare. Mrs. Em's grocery list was there.

"Drew it myself," she announced. "On my walks I sketched those flowers over and over until I could draw them right. Had a lot of trouble with this Blazing Star." She pointed to a five-petaled flower at the end.

"I've never seen one," Sam said. "It's pretty though."

"They open at sunset," Mrs. Em said, "and close in the morning. It has to do with the cool air. They remind me of the horses in a way, appearing morning or evening, living in the most miserable soil." She sighed. "I wish I had the horses in the picture, too, but I never could get them right."

Sam imagined Mrs. Em out early in the morning, waiting behind a juniper, trying to sketch the horses, the way he went out early trying to run better and better. "It's a wonderful picture," he said, "even without the horses." Then he blurted, "Don't you ever get lonesome out here?"

Mrs. Em cut another slice of cake for Sam. "You mean because I talk so much?" she said, laughing. "Might seem that way, but no, I don't get all that lonesome. The country has its moods. Some days it's mean and stingy, and other times it's wild and beautiful. When I get tired of listening to myself talk, I get out my old buggy and go to town." She snapped her fingers. "Say, you want to see my baby?"

"Sure," said Sam without a qualm, cramming the last two bites of cake into his mouth.

He hurried after Mrs. Em, down the front steps and toward the weathered shack. She pulled open one of the double garage doors. Inside was an old black car. Except for a few paint chips, it was shiny clean. She's probably a very careful driver, Sam thought.

"Up ahead here," she said, squeezing past the car.

Sam saw boards stacked sideways, fencing off a corner of the shed, and heard a puppy yapping. However, when he looked down at the small, frisking animal, he wasn't sure whether it was a dog or not. Its ears seemed large for its head and its eyes were almond-shaped.

"Coyote pup," Mrs. Em announced. "Abe Andrews, same fellow who wants my house, shot the mother. Claimed she was raiding his cattle, which is nonsense. Anyway, I set out walking and by pure luck found her two pups. I brought them back here to feed, but one died. This one's healthy and devilish though."

The pup wriggled and tried to jump to her. She reached down to scratch its ears. "Andrews heard about this pup," she told Sam over her shoulder, "and now he wants to shoot it, too. I think I can raise him tame, but Andrews says he'll go wild again first chance."

In the pen, the pup raced back and forth, stumbled, somersaulted and landed with a splash in the water bowl.

"There you go making a mess," said Mrs. Em, laughing as the pup shook himself. She picked him up and cradled him in one arm. The pup tried to lick her. "I made the mistake of giving him a name," she said. "Shouldn't have, of course, it'll make it harder when Andrews comes to shoot him."

Sam reached out timidly to pat the pup. "What do you call it?"

"I named him Don Coyote," she said with a laugh. "It's the Spanish title *Don*, plus their way of saying coyote. And besides, it sounds a little like *Don Quixote*. Have you heard of that Spanish knight and his quest?"

Sam gasped. "A vision quest?"

It was Mrs. Em's turn to be surprised. "Vision quest? Why . . . no . . . he was a knight of high ideals. . . . What vision quest?" She watched Sam closely.

He regretted blurting it out. "I read about one somewhere," he said, faltering. "I think the Indians went on vision quests. I must of read it in history . . . like the tipi rings. I don't know why I thought of it. . . ." He broke off.

Mrs. Em nodded, pursing her lips thoughtfully. "Yes, that's so," she agreed. "There are the remains of what claims to be a vision site up in the mountains. I saw it years ago, under the crest of a bluff, nestled in, with a half circle of rocks in front."

Sam tried to be casual. "That's real interesting." He

bent toward the pup to hide his excitement. "I don't suppose you know where it is now though."

"Certainly I know where it is. I've hiked over every inch of these mountains at some time or other. Before my legs got so old."

"Wouldn't mind seeing it," Sam said casually. "Long as I'm in the area, I mean."

Mrs. Em tucked the pup back inside his pen. "I'll draw you a map," she said, chuckling, "be good for your education, all right. It's six or seven miles beyond the tipi rings, and they're about ten from here, but I can give you a ride that far."

She glanced at her watch. "Tell you what. I'll trade you a good meal for some work. My garden needs weeding, and you can do that while I cook dinner. Then, this afternoon I'll drive you to the tipi rings. What do you say?"

"It's a deal."

In the garden Sam worked carefully on hands and knees, moving up and down the rows, pulling the weeds and tossing them in a basket. Just imagine, he thought, finding a real old vision site. Not even Clete knew about that. I'll go there and sit and sort things through. If I can. Be like getting rid of these weeds. Thinking of it made the whole story real to Sam. If there were such a place, there might be real visions. He felt anxious to be on his way.

He hoed narrow furrows beside each row and made ring furrows around each potato plant. Then he carried pails of water and poured it carefully into these shallow grooves so it sank near the plant roots. It's nice here, he decided, wish mom and I had a garden . . . and all this land to run in. Wish mom could see this. I wonder if she's okay, not too sad.

Mrs. Em gave him a bowl to fill with fresh, ruffly lettuce, and he was pinching off leaves of it when he heard an engine. A pickup truck swung into the driveway and skidded to a stop. The side door groaned open and a tall, bulky man lumbered out. He did not notice Sam kneeling in the garden.

A rack holding a gun hung in the rear window of the pickup. Seeing it, Sam frowned, left the lettuce in a heap and crept closer to the schoolhouse.

Mrs. Em's voice carried through an open side window. "Anyone with a dog as vicious as yours can't talk about wild animals," she said. "If you've lost calves, I'd look at what he has for supper. My pup isn't raiding your herd."

The man's answer was a mumble, but Sam guessed that this was Mr. Andrews, come to shoot the coyote. He glanced at the shed. The front door was still ajar. Seemed unfair to destroy such a small animal.

"Now, Andrews, don't fly off the handle. . . ."

"Fly off the handle!" the man shouted. "So would you if you was losing stock. You want a pet? Get a dog. No coyote ever amounted to a damn." There was movement inside. "Let's finish it and get it over with," said the man.

Sam knew what to do. He sprinted toward the shed,

squeezed through the doorway and hurried to the pen. The pup raised his head, awake instantly, and ventured a wag of his tail. Sam scooped him up in one arm and wrapped his other hand around the muzzle. The pup could breathe, but not yelp.

He heard the pickup door opening again and knew the man was lifting the gun from its rack. Sam kicked a hole in the dirt under the boards, the size of a small pup. Then he darted to the far side of Mrs. Em's car and crouched just as the garage door swung open wide.

"Pen's back in the corner," Mrs. Em said in a tired voice. "Abe, it's just a little pup."

"They get big."

The two edged along the opposite side of the car. Sam moved like a duck, pressing the wriggling pup against him. At the back of the car he hesitated, hoping their attention was on the pen, then waddled around the edge of the closed door.

Once outside, Sam circled the shed to avoid crossing the open door. The hilltop behind the school was too far to reach as a hiding place, so he darted toward the schoolhouse. He cleared the entry steps in two leaps and scrambled inside the front hall. There he wedged behind the door to listen at the crack. The pup kicked furiously, glaring up at Sam.

"Damned funny," said the man's voice, "that pup scratching out under the fence."

"I'm as surprised as you are," said Mrs. Em in a delighted tone. "But I wouldn't have taken you out there if I'd known the pup was gone, would I?" Their voices were coming closer.

"Sure you would," said the man with a chuckle. "That's just what you'd do and all the time have the pup stowed away safe inside. You don't, do you?"

Mrs. Em laughed. "I wish I'd thought of that. Come on in and have a cup of coffee. You can peek in the corners and make sure there's no pup."

"Aw, Mrs. Em, I believe you. Coffee sounds good though. Let me hang this gun back first."

Sam stiffened behind the door. Why hadn't he stayed outside, behind the shed, or hunched under a window? Here he'd be found for sure. And the pup with him.

10

Sam pressed against the wall. Would he be hidden behind the door? His back scraped the rungs of the ladder and he remembered the trapdoor above.

He grabbed the scarf from its hook and tied it fast around the pup's jaw. Now one hand was free to grab a high rung. Hugging the pup in the crook of his elbow allowed his other hand to grasp another rung at chest level. Reach, step, hold; reach, step, hold. In this jerky fashion, he grappled up the ladder.

His reaching hand shoved the light trapdoor open. It swung up, creaking, in a flurry of dust and dead bugs. Sam thrust the pup onto the floor of the belfry. There were sounds on the wooden steps outside.

Sam hauled himself up through the trapdoor, swinging his legs high and inside. He lowered the door shut just as he heard footsteps below.

Beside him the pup scraped at the scarf with his foreleg. Sam lifted the small animal into his lap and scratched between his ears. He checked the scarf to make it firm but not too tight, and kept the pup from rubbing it loose. The animal stared reproachfully at him and finally lay down with his chin on a paw.

Stealthily, Sam stood up so he could see over the sides of the bell tower. Rolling hills stretched on three sides, and the mountains seemed especially close from this lookout. Sam was impatient to reach them. It's good I came, he decided. It's a special thing—this quest. What would Clete say? Probably call me Sam Saves-the-Pup. How about that for a name, Clete? He smiled even while the lump swelled in his throat. Why, he wondered, why couldn't I have saved Clete?

Voices drifted up the tower shaft, but Sam paid no attention until he heard a chair being pushed back. Then he sat back on the floor again, out of sight of the pickup.

"Sorry about all this, Mrs. Em, but that pup would've gone bad sure as anything. As it is, he'll probably starve to death and that's no loss."

"You're all heart, Abe. I don't remember teaching you anything like this."

A short laugh and then, "I just know what's practical. Same as I know it's practical for a lady like you to move into town, close to people and stores and all."

"Don't start that again. I have a lease as long as I care to live here, and I still care to."

"Mrs. Em, don't let anyone tell you you're not stubborn."

Sam resisted the urge to peek over the railing. The truck backed onto the main road and drove away. After a few moments he cautiously stood up.

Mrs. Em was standing by the shed, hands on hips, surveying the field behind the shed. Sam slipped the scarf off the pup's nozzle.

As if uncorked, the pup spilled over, yelping. Mrs. Em swung around, scanning the yard, before she looked up at the tower. Sam waved.

"Oh, you two!" she began. "Did he have some help digging out?"

Sam bowed.

Mrs. Em roared with laughter.

"Heaven's name . . . come on down. That tower floor's as strong as a toothpick."

Climbing down needed less maneuvering than the climb

up. Sam delivered the pup into Mrs. Em's arms, then fixed the trapdoor. There, he thought, I did one thing right.

Inside, Mrs. Em poured two mugs of coffee. "A toast to our victory," she said. The pup attacked a small rug by the door.

"Will he be back?" Sam asked.

"Oh, he drops in from time to time. If he sees the pup, we'll start all over again."

"What will you do?"

She looked down at the pup, who was curling the rug into a nest around himself. "In a few weeks I'll make another pen for him, somewhere out in a field. Close enough so I can feed him but far enough so he gets a taste of freedom. Sooner or later he'll make it out of the pen. Then he'll be back once or twice, and finally he'll be gone. In the wild they're on their own at five or six months." She sighed. "Like any youngster . . . you can help them just so much, then they have to go out on their own."

They sat quietly. Sam considered the pup, who was now asleep. The wild horses survive, he thought, maybe the pup will, too. At least we helped him.

"Well, I'm hungry," Mrs. Em announced. "There's chicken baked in the oven. That sound good to you?"

Sam brought in the lettuce and then he washed up. Mrs. Em spread a yellow tablecloth and smoothed away the fold creases. She placed a glass vase filled with pink cosmos in the center. "Makes it a company dinner," she told him.

Sam tried to eat slowly so she wouldn't know how hungry he really was. For dessert he had another slice of chocolate cake.

Mrs. Em finished and stared thoughtfully out the window. "I do sometimes think of moving into town," she said softly. "Be more convenient in some ways. Andrews can't wait to turn this into a granary." She smiled sadly. "Can you imagine what the ghosts would think of that?"

"Ghosts?"

"Why, a schoolhouse is always haunted," she said. "Everyone who ever passed through left a little bit of his spirit behind to keep me company. This room's crowded with youngsters, just as real sometimes as if they were only outside for recess."

Sam glanced furtively around the room. She sure said some strange things, he thought again.

"Those steps outside are full of ghosts, too," she went on, thinking aloud. "Some of the best classes were there on the steps. Late afternoon, when no one wanted to study, we'd pick up and go out. We made a game of it. The steps were our boat and a book or poem was the ticket and we were off to explore. Course the exploring was inside their heads, they were too poor for real travel —not like kids today. But they went as far in many ways. We read Twain and Stevenson and even some of *Don Quixote* and his quest. . . ." She broke off. "Which reminds me, we'd better get you started."

She stacked the dishes and draped a dish towel over them. "I don't want to do them, and I sure don't want to look at them," she said. "I'll pack a lunch for you, seeing how you're traveling so light. Perhaps you're carrying a load I can't see. Your folks don't mind you tramping off alone?"

Sam tensed. Might have known she'd get to this. "It's just my mom and me," he said. "My father's dead." True so far and it sounded right. "She's away right now . . . and I thought to do some exploring. My friend told me about the tipi rings." He didn't know what else to say.

"Nothing wrong with seeing a little of the world," Mrs. Em agreed, opening the high-backed kitchen cabinet. "A boy needs some growing room once in a while . . . long as you're sensible about it."

She made bread-and-butter sandwiches and slipped them into a plastic bag. Then she filled a pint jar with dark, steaming coffee and capped it. "Be cold when you drink it, but it'll be wet." She yanked open the refrigerator. "Some cheese," she said to herself, "and an orange."

"That's plenty. Too much," Sam protested.

"Got homemade raisin cookies," she continued, ignoring him, "and I'll wrap up a chicken leg and that's probably as much as you want to carry. Think you'll be all right?"

"I could last a week," he said.

She walked to the blackboard and erased the shopping list with a quick swipe. "Now, here's the map."

"The schoolhouse," she drew an X, "and here's the road out front, which we follow until it meets the county road running north to Box Elder, that's in the next state. We cross the county road and take a cow path in toward the tipi rings, which are here." She added circles and made a meandering diagonal line above them. "This canyon's deep and the Little Crow River runs through. It's not so high now, but in a rain, with all the draws feeding it, it floods in seconds. You wouldn't believe a flash flood unless you'd seen one."

She sketched several rows of triangles above the river line. "The mountains begin slam on the other side of the river," she said. "Be ready for some real climbing. Those boots you're wearing are terrible for hiking, but I don't have anything to give you."

Turning back to the map, she put a dotted line from the circles through the triangles. "Cross Little Crow gulch and reach the first hilltops and you'll see a fair-sized mountain off to your left. There'll be a long oval opening on top, like a needle's eye. Actually it's two tall boulders sitting side by side, but from this angle they look joined on top. The Indians called it 'Cave in the Clouds.' Farther into the mountains, you won't see the needle's eye, just the rocks.

"Go on north," she extended the dotted line, "until you come upon a catch basin. The government built it to hold water for the wild herds. I haven't seen it myself, since I stopped hiking so far, but it's supposed to be about here. About halfway." She drew a rectangular shape. "Say, keep your eye open for Belle. She's been known to range up and down Little Crow gulch."

Sam watched every stroke she made and memorized every word.

"When you reach the catch basin, angle to the left, toward the highest peak you can see; that's where the vision site is. If you were to strike off to the right, you'd come out on the rim of Big Crow River canyon. What a sight! Takes my breath away remembering it. But you don't want to go that way, and anyway, you'll get almost the same view when you're high up on the vision site."

She turned back to the map. "After a mile or so north of the catch basin, you'll find a small stream. It's named Gyp Creek, and it's narrow but deep enough to always have water. Follow upstream until the river bends north. From there you walk straight west, overland, to the base of the mountain. The vision site is scooped out under the crest."

She dropped the chalk in its tray. "Don't I wish I could come with you!" She studied the map again. "On to the north, following the creek, you'd come out somewhere in the next state. There are no roads crisscrossing the mountains, just the country road running north as I said. Well, you're anxious to go. I would be."

She rummaged through the trunk in the hall and returned carrying a denim shirt. "Some kid left this here once. It'll fit you for a jacket. Gets cold up there." She placed the shirt on the table and piled the food in the center. Then she wrapped the food inside and tied it all shut with the sleeves. "How's that for a pack?" she asked, grinning. "We'll hang it on my old umbrella and you're fit as a hobo."

"Not the umbrella!"

"Why sure, be good for a sunshade or windscreen or tent top or even in case of rain . . . whatever rain is." She slipped the pack over the handle and gave it all to Sam.

He lifted it reluctantly. There wasn't ever, he thought, an Indian on a vision quest with an umbrella.

"Let's get the car. The afternoon's half gone," said Mrs. Em.

"What if I lose this umbrella?" It was his last hope.

"What if you do," she said. "No great loss. I doubt you will, and you can drop it off here when you come back. That way I'll hear about your adventure. Or if you don't come by here, why you can leave it at any ranch or some store in Vista. Everybody knows me. I'll get the umbrella back sooner or later."

At the garage, Sam pushed open the doors, and Mrs. Em carried the pup back to his pen. "Behave yourself," she told him, boarding up the hole.

Mrs. Em backed the car onto the gravel road so fast Sam held his breath. Maybe she's nervous backing up, he thought, so she does it in a hurry. She shoved the clutch into gear and the car lunged forward. Gravel hailed under the fenders. Sam gripped the armrest and watched the electric poles flash by. In the corner of his eye he saw Mrs. Em's chin jutted forward, her eyes narrowed on the road. She was all business.

Six miles later, as they approached the higher grade of the county gravel road, she asked, "Anyone coming your way?"

"Nobody I can see." Sam looked wildly in both directions.

"Okay!" With a roar the car leaped onto the higher road and pitched directly down the opposite bank onto a dirt path. She had called it a path. Wheel tracks were barely visible in the weeds and grass. "Not many people come this way," she said. Sam believed it.

Her car lurched over the bumpy roadbed, winding through foothills streaked brick-red and pink. The path finally emerged onto a patchy tableland where large rocks jutted up among the dun and green and gold of the grasses.

"This is as close as we'll drive," said Mrs. Em, slamming on the brakes. "It's rough from here on."

Sam gulped. "I'd of thought that would be a challenge for you," he ventured.

Mrs. Em laughed. "There are those who say I drive too fast. I hope you're not one of them." She bounded out of the car. Sam planted both feet on the ground and steadied his hand on the door as he got out.

"The best view of these tipi rings is from an airplane,"

Mrs. Em was saying. "Unfortunately, we don't have one, but you'll get the idea if you study the layout." She gestured with a sweep of her arm.

Near them was a circle of large rocks, eight or ten feet in diameter. In the field beyond, Sam glimpsed more and more rocks among the grass. Moving closer he saw that the circles repeated all across the flatland. "How many are there?" he gasped.

"Oh, I don't really know. Easily one hundred, I believe. It might have been the campsite for several tribes. Some say the rocks were used to fasten the base of the tipi when the ground was too frozen to drive in stakes. You can see that, besides being round themselves, the tipis were grouped in a circle, a symbol for the tribes. Even the ceremonial dances followed the circle. Their sacred objects were circles: the sun, the moon, the earth around them."

"The sacred hoop!" Sam said. "I know about that. I know a man, says his Indian grandfather told about a camp in the mountains. Maybe it was this very one. Maybe he lived in this very circle."

"Maybe," Mrs. Em said. "Imagine it filled with tipis, smoke curling up from the fires, children playing in the fields. People coming and going, finding game, cooking it. Why, it's as full of ghosts as my old schoolhouse, don't you think?"

Sam wished she hadn't even mentioned it. "Hmmm," he said.

"This was a full culture, even though it seemed poor to people who came later. They didn't see the strengths. How the Indians revered the land, for instance. How they valued physical courage and endurance. And how . . . oh, listen to me. Put a nickle in a teacher and out comes a dollar lecture."

Sam was listening. "Is that what that Spanish knight believed, too?"

"Don Quixote? It wasn't quite the same. He was a knight in search of wrongs to be righted. Well, come to think of it, I'm sure he would have taken up for the Indians."

They stood looking across the open field. Empty as it was, Sam had a prickly feeling on the back of his neck, as if he were being watched.

Finally Mrs. Em said, "I'll be getting home now. You remember the map?"

Sam nodded.

"I should have written it out for you!" She searched her pockets for a paper scrap. "I'm so accustomed to that blackboard."

"I remember."

"Yes. Well . . . go have a look. The mountains are beautiful. It should be an adventure." She admired the slopes to the north. "Needs a youngster to start a trip like that."

She nodded at him sternly. "Pay attention to direction. Should take you until noon tomorrow to reach the vision site. It's six or seven miles, but it's all up and down, slow going. And then a half day getting back . . . and, oh . . . you should reach my place about noon the next day . . . if you come by. I expect even my cooking will be inviting by then."

"Thanks for the help," Sam said. He suddenly thought of telling her about his own quest. He stammered, "Maybe I'll see a vision . . . like the Indian boys. . . ."

Mrs. Em laughed. "Those visions aren't just waiting around like altitude spots before your eyes. An Indian boy fasted and went through physical pain . . . not to mention the wear and tear on his nerves . . . in order to see a vision. Let's hope you have an easier trip. Stand up straight now." She looked at him critically. "Use your head and keep your directions."

She walked to her car without looking back. With only a wave she turned the car around and shot off down the path.

Sam was alone.

||

He stood in the center of the ghost camp. A breeze bobbed the grass, whispering in his ears. Several times he wondered if someone were behind him. Not a ghost, he didn't believe that. A rider, perhaps. But each time he turned, the sound blew silently away.

There were no eyes to see him, just as there were no whispers, but he imagined them. Somewhere. Beady and accusing, like the dead coyote's stare; almost a warning.

If I had been a boy here, Sam thought, I would know stories about the vision quests. I wonder how many other boys have gone out from here. . . . I wonder what they found . . . and how they felt.

Sam picked up the umbrella and pack and slung it hobo-style over his shoulder. He walked stealthily between the circles of stones as if someone slept there still.

At the edge of the campsite, a cutbank plunged sharply to the riverbed. Sam slid most of the way down. There was a shallow flow of water in the center of the river, but the sides were dry and rocky. Sam jumped the water. Little Crow River, he repeated to himself, and Big Crow is to the east.

The bank beside him was steep, and overhead were bowl-shaped mud nests built by the bank swallows. He trailed beside the river until finally he hooked the umbrella over the back of his belt and clambered up the bank, grabbing onto clumps of grass.

Behind was the flat field of the tipi rings. Below, the swallows swooped in and out of their homes. Sam looked for the needle's-eye mountain, but all he saw was another hill directly before him.

He began climbing carefully, eyes on the slope, when

a small avalanche of rocks spilled down beside him. He straightened to find the old mare, Belle, peering quizzically down at him.

"Hello, old girl," Sam said softly, grinning with pleasure. "Mrs. Em said I might meet you." The horse tossed her head as if sniffing his words. Then she wheeled, switched her tail and disappeared beyond the hilltop.

Sam scrambled after her and found her standing sideways, watching for him.

"Wait up," Sam said. "Keep me company. First thing is to get my bearings." He shadowed his eyes against the lowering sun. The landmark mountain rose high and sharp in the distance. "Cave in the Clouds," he whispered, impressed by the giant oval eye at its peak. "Right where it should be, Belle. Sitting way over west."

The mare whickered softly, as if agreeing with him.

"Let's make tracks," said Sam. He shouldered his pack and started down the hillside, slamming his bootheels into the soft earth.

Belle picked her way daintily down the slope and took the lead across the meadowland, sashaying between the tall spires of sage. Sam clomped after, wishing his boots weren't hot and heavy.

"If you used to be tame," he said to the horse, "how about giving me a lift? No point in both of us walking."

The next hill looked steep and rough-going. Sam was wondering how to hike it when he saw Belle moving diagonally up the slope. Tracking her, Sam found a ledge, uneven but wide enough to walk on. Private road, wild horses only, Sam thought.

Partway up, the path switched back to the opposite diagonal. Sam's knees ached. He wanted to rest, but he also wanted Belle in his sights. The horse plodded ahead, and Sam hitched along behind, taking deeper and deeper gasps of air.

When the trail crested the hill, Sam discovered his legs hurt as much going downhill as up. The hill bottomed out in a basin of a higher elevation than the one before. Sam's breath felt lighter. He wanted to rest before tackling the next slope, but it seemed easier to follow Belle than to pick his own way.

He mopped his brow and along his temples and tasted salt when he rubbed his hand across his lips. Late afternoon sunlight reflecting off the bare soil stung his eyes. A nice shady juniper, he thought, that would be okay. Or a splash in a cool river. When I come to the catch basin, I'll just roll downhill and right up to my neck in water.

Can't be far, the way Mrs. Em drew that map. I feel right at home here. Everything lies the way I pictured it. Easy as crossing my own backyard.

He craned his neck to sight on Belle, but the mare was gone. She's over the ridge, he thought, puffing. Never mind, I'll find her. Maybe she saw the water and ran down for a drink. Whew . . . move over, horse.

But when Sam lumbered to the top, he flopped to the ground, eyes closed. You'll have to wait for me, Belle, he thought. This is as far as I go for a while. He felt hot enough to melt, and there seemed to be small explosions of color inside his eyelids.

When he opened his eyes, the horse was not in the valley below or drinking at the water's edge. There was no water, no catch basin. There was baked, cracked earth needing rain.

Sam stared down the hill, frowning. She's pulled into a draw somewhere, he thought. She couldn't disappear like a ghost. Funny I haven't come onto that catch basin, if my directions are straight.

He faced west, scanning the peaks for the needle's eye. He found nothing resembling it, not even a rocky mass that he knew for sure was the Cave in the Clouds.

The sense of being in his own backyard vanished, leaving Sam tired clear through. He stretched out against the ground. Maybe Belle will come back, he thought, once it's cooler.

He rolled onto his stomach and looked in the direction he had come. He was high enough to see over the ridges behind him, to the red buttes bordering them and to the small, white smudge that was the town of Vista.

Beyond the grassy plains to the south, though he could not see it, was his hometown, his own too-quiet house. He remembered his mother's face as she spoke of his father. And Clete's hollowed cheeks, his mouth twisting to speak. Sam shuddered.

It was your story, Clete, Sam thought, and your grandfather that left it to you, but it's me out here. I'm going to be at the center of the hoop of the world for a while, just for a while, to get things straight.

He tried to remember how this day had begun, early in the cool dawn. There had been the horse Belle and then the herd with the beautiful buckskin . . . and Mrs. Em . . . and . . . Heavy with heat and fatigue, he fell asleep.

The breeze, strong in late afternoon, died as the sun dipped behind the peaks. Shadows edged up from the ravine to where Sam lay. On the ridgeline opposite, three horses trailed single file toward a waterhole. The lead horse was ghost-white in the twilight.

Sam woke shivering in the cooling air, confused by the shapes surrounding him and the strange speckles of light overhead.

The mountains, he remembered, watching the dark masses. And the stars! He marveled at how close they seemed. One cluster of low stars puzzled him until he realized they were the lights of Vista. I must be asleep, he thought, to make that mistake.

He untied the food bundle and eagerly pulled on the jacket. Then he ate the chicken and two sandwiches and drank mouthfuls of cold coffee.

The sky darkened as the full moon rose. Sam considered moving on by moonlight, but one look at the black hollows below changed his mind. I'm not in such a rush, he decided.

Besides, it was lovely and quiet where he was. Sam gazed up at the silent peaks and the stars. What was it Clete said? What the Indians called . . . Sam remembered, it meant . . . Great Mystery. That was it. I like that. It feels right: Great Mystery.

It came to him in a rush: that funeral was today. It's over. Mom might be on her way home. She'll be tired. Should have left a note so she wouldn't worry. She wouldn't think much of this, I bet.

Then Sam smiled into the darkness. Course if Clete could see me now . . . he'd say, "Shoot, if he ain't the foolest kid. Gonna call him Sam Head in the Clouds." But I wouldn't care, Clete, even if you called me Many Troubles.

Sam stretched out again, intending to watch the sky and follow his thoughts, but soon he drifted into sleep. He did not hear the scurry of the pack rat rifling his bundle for the cheese and cookies. Only a lucky mumble in his sleep frightened off another scrounger and saved the orange.

12

Sam pounded the ground with his fist. "Why didn't I build rocks over it?" he asked himself. He picked a smooth, white stone from the cheese wrappings, apparently a trade, and threw it as far as he could. But the bag of cookie crumbs made him laugh. Cleaned out about as flat as Albert, he thought.

He rewrapped the coffee jar and the orange in his jacket and slid it onto the umbrella handle. At home, he thought, I'd be getting up to run. Bud would like it if he ever tried it. Course it cools off in the evening, too, and we wouldn't have to run so far, not at first. I never thought, but I could run in the morning alone and run in the evening with Bud. I guess I kind of shut him off. Maybe if I met him halfway, we'd get to be friends.

Lost in thought, Sam slipped in the loose shale and sat with a plop, barely missing a prickly pear. After that he watched his footing carefully, picking his way across the ravine.

He hoped to discover the catch basin in the next valley. Not that he doubted he would find it. Even if Mrs. Em hasn't actually seen the catch basin, he told himself, it's sure to be there. Probably over the next hill.

Near the top, a snuffle made him stop and listen. Might be Belle, he thought. She spooks me often enough, maybe I can sneak up on her this time.

Sam crouched close to the hill and crept forward along a narrow ledge which skirted an outcropping of rock. Sam did not see the far slope until he came crawling onto it. Then it was too late. He was ten feet from a leathery, wild stallion.

The horse whinnied an alarm. Sam froze on hands and knees. He was close enough to count the muscle cords in the horse's powerful legs. From the corner of his eye, Sam saw three mares and a colt stop grazing in the valley below. The catch basin was a gray-blue reflection behind them.

The stallion tossed his head, wild-eyed, snorting commands to the lead mare. Sam's mouth went dry. He saw the mare move out, followed by the others.

I can't back up, Sam realized, never find that skinny ledge. The stallion lunged one way, then the other, wheeling in a screen of dust. He reared and flailed out with his hooves. He's fixing to clobber me, Sam thought.

With an angry cry, the horse hurtled toward him. Sam watched it come, spellbound. At the last minute, he flopped forward, hugging his arms over his head. The earth jarred under him and his nose stung with dust.

The slicing hooves sounded again, but softer, farther away. Sam barely lifted his head to peer down the slope. The stallion was racing through the gulch after his harem.

Slowly Sam sat up and watched the horse disappear over the far hilltop. Now that the threat was gone, he began to tremble.

"That big fellow just wanted to scare me," Sam said in a squeaky voice. He did it, too, Sam thought, but at least I've found the catch basin. I'm halfway.

Sam stumbled down to the water's edge. The ground was powder-soft and marked with hoofprints. He glanced around nervously and knelt. He cupped his hands and splashed water on his face. Then he uncapped the coffee and drank it in one long swallow. Take some water here, he told himself, until I find fresher. Better start making tracks of my own. No sense hanging around here. He looked over his shoulder, but there were no more horses.

The next slope was gentle, and from the crest he sighted the herd, faraway, dark shapes dotting the shrubs and boulders. Just wanted to scare me, Sam thought again. Guarding his band. Otherwise they might wind up in a corral or dog food. It was something . . . that was one blustery horse! Like one of Clete's stories. Only, it's mine.

Ahead, hilltops rose like steps of a giant staircase. One peak bulked over the others. That's it, Sam thought, that's where I'll find the vision site. Looks to be a narrow canyon running toward it. I see treetops from here, so I know there's water. Must be Gyp Creek. The way the map read, I follow the creek almost to the base of the mountain.

Wonder what it'll be like up there, Sam thought. Should I sing a song or make a prayer or what. One thing sure, I'll be hungry. He rubbed a hand over his stomach.

The sun rose high as Sam hiked. He was glad to slide

down the steep canyon slope toward the shade trees, and he heard the stream even before he saw it. The water twinkled in the sunlight, so clear Sam could see the stones that lined the bottom. Floating in quiet pockets along the banks were clumps of water buttercups, mossy-green dotted with white blossoms.

Sam hauled off his boots and socks and hopped into the water. Instantly the icy current sliced at his feet. "Yeeeoow!" he yelled, leaping out.

"Gyp Creek?" he sputtered. "Frozen Foot Creek!"

He stamped his tingling feet until they were dry, then pulled on his socks and wedged his feet back into his boots. Won't have to cool them off again, he thought. Finally, he refilled the jar with the clear water, wrapped it in his pack and moved off upstream.

The tall peak was hidden from his view, and after a mile or more, when the creek angled off to the right, Sam climbed the bank to check his bearings. He almost cheered to find the vision peak close, sitting regally among the lower hills.

A stretch of shallow basin land lay between him and the base of the peak. Not long now, he promised himself.

He dodged between waist-high sagebrush, eyeing the ground for any long reptile with a rattle for a tail. He shifted the umbrella from one shoulder to the other but stubbornly refused to open it as a shade.

When the basin land began its sharp rise toward the

mountain, Sam ducked under a scrub juniper to rest. The mountain looked forbidding. He could not see the peak from this angle, so he sighted on a ridge about a third of the way. I'll eat the orange there, he thought.

Sam tackled the lower slope with the umbrella and pack flopping from the back of his belt. The earth was hot to touch where he grabbed handholds. It slid under his boots.

"Okay, you mountain," Sam whispered, "I've gotten this far." He edged up slowly until he could flatten his hands on the ridge he had sighted from below and haul himself onto it. He twisted into a sitting position, rubbing his sore palms. From the top, the hill seemed even steeper than from the bottom.

When Sam lifted his eyes to the view, he forgot how tired he was. The far banks of Big Crow canyon wound for miles under a lavender haze. The river, where he glimpsed it, was turquoise. The foothills beyond rose and fell in ocean patterns. They seemed to float endlessly back to some remote corner of the world.

A breeze up from the canyon cooled his face. Feeling content, Sam drew the orange from his pack and bit into the skin. He peeled off a thick slice and tossed it away. It landed near his foot like a bright piece of litter. He scuffed dirt over it, but he shoved the rest of the peelings into his pocket.

He popped a juicy section of orange into his mouth.

Even Mina's pies didn't taste as sweet. He ate slowly, making it last. He took a long drink from the water jar and stood up.

Above his ledge, the mountain rose steeply for half of the way, then eased back. The peak curved high and out, like a wave hung in full motion.

Sam wedged the umbrella into a crevice and stowed the water jar with it to make climbing easier. He tied the jacket around his waist. The steep, open slope was hard-packed by wind and ribbed with tiny rain gullies. Sam kicked toeholds with his boots. These pointed boots are good for something, he thought.

He inched up, grasping large rocks for hand support. About fifteen feet above the trail he found a boulder large enough to lean against. A glance at the ledge below left him dizzy. It seemed pencil-thin with a steep plunge below. He swung his eyes toward the crest. It's close, he promised himself.

He stretched his right hand toward a spindly spruce growing between two rocks, but his fingertips barely touched the rough bark. His left hand was flat against the hillside with no firm grip.

Below the spruce Sam saw a long slab of shale, as inviting as a carved step, and he slid his foot up and onto it. He shifted his weight.

There was a soft crack no louder than a rip. The slab under his foot split even with the ground. Off-balance and with only a fingerhold, he pitched sideways.

His right knee smacked a rock. His hands raked blindly for something to grab. Stones slashed his arms and face as he plunged down the slope. His eyes squeezed shut.

He landed with a crack on the trail below, whacking his knee again, his ankle folded beneath him.

"Aiiiiieeee," he cried, dragging breath between his teeth. For a moment he lay dazed, and then he struggled to sit up.

Gingerly he drew his knee up, cupping his hands about the pain. After many minutes he flexed the knee. Not broken, he thought, not if it bends. He massaged it, waiting for the pain to stop.

At last he pushed himself onto his feet. He favored the injured knee, putting weight on it gradually. It'll be sore, he thought. My ankle, too, where I landed on it. But the knee moves; it's not broken.

Sam began again, working his way up the slippery slope. He gripped the largest rocks, tested each footing. His knee hurt if he pressed against it, but he did not stop.

Twice his ankle faltered, but Sam blamed it on loose bits of shale. At the large boulder, he pulled up and grimly wiped away the sweat blurring his eyes. "I'll make it," he muttered.

The slope was in late-afternoon shadow now, and Sam moved, tense and cautious, remembering the long skid to the bottom. His hands ached from clutching the rocks.

Once he dragged himself waist-high against a shelf of rock and rolled onto it. It was no wider than a bale of hay, but Sam sprawled gratefully, arms and legs shaking.

Some climb, he thought, make a mountain goat shake. I feel so chilly, too, must be the shade. He rose stiffly and turned toward the peak. Its arched crest seemed more like a wave than ever. The bank dropped sharply in front, but from the side the approach was a gentle rise. Sam walked favoring his right leg.

Under the arch was a shallow natural cave, high enough and wide enough to sit inside. A semicircle of rocks, piled double, marked the front. Sam hesitated. All those boys who have been here before, he thought, maybe they wouldn't like it, me being here.

Then he ducked inside the border of rocks and squatted with his legs crossed under him. The rock slab at his back was cold to lean against and the air seemed damp. Sam untied the jacket and pulled it on. The same rolling scene of hills into plains into sky lay before him. No, he decided, those boys wouldn't mind. They'd share this. I feel it.

"In the hoop of the world," he whispered. "I made it, Clete. Took a while and I'm beat up, but I'm here. You'd like it. You could pick a ranch from here." Sam felt as close to the old man as if Clete had suddenly stretched out beside him, rummaging in his overall pocket for a chaw. Thinking of his old friend, Sam's eyes and throat stung and he squeezed his hands into helpless fists.

A long sigh escaped him and he yearned to lie down. Just for a couple minutes, he promised himself. I feel run out. Little snooze is all I need.

Curling inside the cave, Sam settled himself as comfortably as he could. "In the hoop of the world," he repeated. Around him only the tops of the hills still caught the sunlight. Long shadow fingers filled the canyons and reached up the draws. He was asleep by the time the moon rose. Even the cold mountain air did not wake him.

Much later, however, his sleep became restless. An ache made him shift his leg one way and another. He mumbled softly. The ache grew sharper.

13

As he slept, Sam's body stiffened against the pain. The sound of his own moans woke him. His muscles began to shiver until his whole body shook, and he wrapped his arms across his chest to hold himself warm and quiet.

He thought, is it my knee? Can't be my knee. What if it's broken? Can't be broken. I walked on it after I fell.

The shivering increased. His teeth clattered, but Sam couldn't stop them. Numbing cold seeped into every part of him.

Move, he told himself, move. Get warm. Struggling,

Sam managed to lean against the stone backrest. He ground his teeth together to stop their chatter. Slowly he realized that the pain was not from his knee but surging up from a little hollow below his anklebone.

"I twisted it," he whispered, "but it didn't hurt till now."

Sam still wore his boots for warmth, but he needed to pull off the right one to free his ankle. He strained at the bootheel, trying to straighten his foot inside the boot to make it slide more easily. The boot would only be moved a half inch at a time. When Sam finally worked it free, he was dizzy from the pain.

Even in the moonlight and with his sock on, Sam knew the ankle was swollen. He tapped it gingerly.

"It swoll up under my boot," he muttered. "That's what made it pound so. Must be sprained. I wonder, can I stand?"

He stretched his hands to the sides for support and wobbled up onto his left foot. Carefully he shifted weight onto the right foot.

The ankle twinged but held. Leave the boot off, he decided, settling back into the alcove.

When the first wan, gray light showed in the east, Sam tugged the sock down over his heel. The swelling was plum-colored, mottled and pulsing under his fingertips. He didn't like the look of it. He pulled the sock back on and arranged his foot on the rocks, hoping to ease the throbbing.

An awesome quiet spread through the canyons below; the moisture clouds hung over the draws like smoke from altar candles. Sam realized that this was the beginning of his vision quest.

Don't suppose a vision would be any prettier, he thought. I feel good here, except for my ankle, and that's sure to get better. Feels like I've done something for Clete, something special. Wonder what he'd say. He never found such a place, I bet. I wonder if my father ever did. If he ran off feeling all raw inside like I did, then he'd need a place like this. I wonder.

Sam's unhappiness edged back. He tried to ignore the nudges from his stomach, and he shifted his swollen ankle on the cold rocks. He wondered if it should be wrapped. Then he took off his jacket long enough to peel out of his tee shirt. This he folded into a fat strip and wound firmly around the ankle, tucking the end securely. That'll keep it warm, he thought, so it won't get stiff. Maybe the swelling will go down.

As the morning sun filled his cubicle, he grew warm and drowsy. Half asleep, he once again climbed the peak. Stretching . . . reaching . . . until in a flash he was falling, scraping over rocks, calling aloud.

He woke with a shout. His ankle was aching and his body was rigid. He tried turning the ankle slowly right and left. Moving it caused pain to streak up his leg.

A bad sprain, he told himself again. Worse than I thought. Sam's mouth was dry and he was growing light-headed, as if his eyes wouldn't focus. I'm as woozy as if I'd run too far, he thought. Wish I had that water jar for a cool sip of Gyp Creek.

The creek! Of course . . . if my ankle keeps hurting, I'll go back and soak it in the creek. . . . That'll take the swelling down.

Having a plan steadied him, and he looked around to get his mind off the ache. A pale stone caught his eye, and he reached for it outside the semicircle. When he opened his palm to examine it, he found the rock held the fluted shape of a perfectly formed seashell. He traced the outline with his fingertips.

"A sea fossil," he breathed, "way up here." What's it mean? A lucky charm? Clete had said a spirit helper gave a boy something to bring him power.

Overhead the crest arched outward. Across the far canyon, the ridgeline seemed rippled in long, undulating waves. Sam wiped his hand across his aching forehead as if to brush away a dizzy sensation. Not a ridge, he thought, it's a giant wave, a fossil wave.

"The sea was here," he said in a loud voice. He stared at the shape in the rock, floating before his eyes.

"Must be my headache," he mumbled, "acting this way . . . a drink of water would fix me up."

No, not the sea . . . it's heat wobbles, Sam thought. A hot day. The impression of vast, moving swells came stronger than ever.

Sam squeezed his eyes shut. Waves seemed to break

into the canyon below, pushing up against the hill, ring-ing in his ears.

"My ankle," he muttered. "It hurts again." Dizzy as he was, Sam knew his confusion began with the pain.

Hurts worse, he decided. Go back to the river. I'm not running out. . . . I'll come up again . . . soon as my ankle's better.

Sam shoved the shell rock in his jacket pocket and crawled over the border of rocks. He clamped his boot under one arm. For when I climb back, he told himself. I have to climb back. Go down slow and easy. Careful with the ankle.

He inched along, favoring the injured leg. Even so, each bump was as sharp as a kick, and by the time he reached the ledge, he was trembling from a cold sweat.

Sam gulped water from the jar and splashed more onto his face. Feels better, he thought, maybe all I needed was a drink.

But as sure as his ankle and his headache throbbed, Sam knew he had to reach the river. He decided to leave the water jug and his boot until he could return. But the umbrella gave him an idea. It would make a runner, a cushion over the rocks.

He slid the umbrella under his leg and heel. Then he looped his belt twice around both bandage and umbrella and buckled it. The umbrella handle curved up where he could guide the runner.

Sliding, pushing with his good leg and one arm, Sam

began the descent. For a while the umbrella did help until loose rock sent him skidding. He braked with his free hand, but not enough. Instinctively he grabbed out with both arms, releasing the umbrella. The tip caught in a crevice, twisting the shaft sideways. Sam's ankle twisted with it. In this position he slid to a stop, crying out with pain. The umbrella lay free beside him. His ankle rested at an odd angle.

Sam looked at the ankle and gagged. Get to the creek, he thought, get cold water on it. Cold water's good for a sprain. His head pounded.

The basin land would have been an easy walk, but it was a long way to crawl. With the umbrella as a cane, he balanced on his left leg and bent his right leg to hold the swollen ankle off the ground.

Sam tried a single hop. The ankle flopped and pain shot up his leg. Still, hop by hop, he stumped across. Sweat dripped down his face; his left leg quivered from his weight. The basin seemed as wide as the Sahara. He looked neither right nor left but at the ground ahead of each hop. Tiny, parched cracks twisted between the sagebrush.

At the first rise he eased to the ground and pushed himself up backward, dragging the injured leg as gently as possible.

On the hilltop he again braced on the umbrella to hop down sideways, eager once he saw the river. He slid down the last bank to the water.

Sam cupped his hand for an icy drink. Jets of sunlight reflected green and white among the water buttercups. The colors swam before his eyes.

Sam unwound the bandage. The ankle throbbed great sickening beats that made him giddy. Gonna hurt, he thought, that cold water.

The boy swung his limp foot out over the water and lowered it slowly. For a moment he felt nothing, only a pleasant coolness. And then the chill mountain water woke nerves deep in his swollen flesh. Sam groaned. He saw flashes of green and white before he passed out.

14

Half conscious, Sam had dreams enough for a dozen visions. Clete's lined face merged with winding canyon walls. Sam's mother moved along a narrow trail, then vanished. Sam reached out for her and plunged forward.

He grabbed to save himself. His hand swatted something as coarse and tangled as a mane. His fingers twisted about the hairs and held. He seemed to rise on the back of a wild horse until suddenly his foot was caught by a pain as sharp as a pitchfork stabbing it. He opened his eyes.

A thick, white cloud drifted across the noontime sky.

His hand grasped a clump of weeds. Sam pulled himself up, groggy, staring at the water. No pitchfork there, but an icy grip. He shuddered and pulled the foot free. The ankle, still swollen, was numb with cold. He edged away from the water and waited, wondering what to do.

More clouds came, trailing patchy shadows along the canyon. Sam wished he had some food. He hadn't eaten since . . . since yesterday. Then he remembered the orange peels in his pocket and dug them out. The first one was tough to chew and left his tongue smarting. He dunked the next in water and ate that, too. Before long, he had eaten all the peelings.

The sight of his puffy, discolored ankle frightened him. Face it, he admitted, I can't climb back to the vision site on that. Or even get the water jar and my boot. No point kidding myself.

You got me into this, Clete, Sam thought with sudden anger. I wouldn't be here if you hadn't told me that story . . . and if . . .

"Don't blame Clete," he said. "I got me into this." No ducking trouble this time. He had to face it out where he was. "Think now. Think what to do."

Which way? Downstream comes to Big Crow canyon, west is the vision site. If I find where I met Gyp Creek and head south, I should come out at Little Crow and the tipi rings. Lots of climbing between here and there. Can't mistake my directions, not the shape my ankle's in.

Sam rewound the tee-shirt bandage and, for extra support, looped his belt in a figure eight around the foot and ankle and buckled it. He hoisted himself up with the umbrella and began hopping beside the creek bed.

At the first bend of the river he doused water on his face and neck. Clouds now covered the sky and the air felt sticky. The jarring hops traveled up his leg to his back. In time his shoulders hurt as if he were hauling bales of hay. "A little more," he said grimly. "I can do a little more."

When the riverbed narrowed between high banks, Sam had to pick his way over loose rocks slowly, to keep his balance. Even so, the umbrella tip sank in sand hidden along the bottom, and he pitched forward, sprawling flat. His pants knee ripped on a jagged rock; the jolt to his ankle made his head spin. He half crawled, half dragged himself off the rocks.

Sam wiped away a trickle of blood from his knee and brushed at his eyes with a shaky hand. The sultry air in the small canyon weighed on him, sluggish and heavy. He wanted never to move. Surely he had followed this river far enough, he thought. It must be time to turn south.

Beside him the slope was high and steep, but on top juniper branches waved, promising a breeze. He began crawling up the slope, thinking how cool the breeze would be. Both knees were rubbed raw as Sam strained to reach the junipers.

At the top the air smelled of rain. Sam wondered

vaguely what time it was. Seems like a week since I slid down from that mountain, he thought. Gray clouds made it as dark as twilight. He rolled onto his back against the ground, arms spread wide.

I hope it rains, he thought. I hope it rains right into my mouth.

He closed his eyes and fell into exhausted sleep. Lightning zigzagged over far peaks, drawing steadily closer. It was about an hour before the thunder woke him.

Make tracks, Sam told himself, storm's coming. Move while there's light.

Even as he strained to stand, lightning snapped like a whip overhead. Thunder boomed around him. It's already closer than I figured, he realized, guess it wouldn't hurt to rest my leg a bit longer. Take shelter and wait it out. Except . . . I'll never find my way at night. Even now it doesn't look like the same land I covered yesterday. Maybe I should go on now, as long as it's not raining yet. Go as far as I can.

Hopping downhill, his good leg seemed all knots. "Hang on," Sam said. "A little farther." He did not see the point at which the land began to rise again, but his exhausted leg felt it. Finally he dropped to the ground to massage it.

Sam tried to console himself. My muscles hurt lots of times when I run. They cramp up and I have to rub them . . . but never quite this bad.

I'll go a little more, he decided grimly, and then wait out the night. Gloomy light obscured everything. He finished the trip on hands and knees, dragging the umbrella beside him. He crawled toward the black hump of a juniper and found his way under the branches. Gratefully he stretched along the ground, arranging the injured ankle as best he could.

He felt used up, drained. Even screaming muscles did not keep him awake. Once he woke in the darkness, stiff and cramped. A cold wind lashed the branches and scattered the clouds. Sam saw moonlight reflected along their edges like slim, pale birds. But if they were birds of a vision, bearing power, he didn't feel it. Or even wonder about it. He lay shivering and sneezing, slapping his arms and thighs to warm up. Only his bandaged ankle seemed hot.

His stomach felt like drying rawhide. He fingered through the prickly needles for the blue juniper berries he had seen by day. They were bitter to chew, almost overpowering, and they burned his stomach. He ate as many as he found.

He tried to remember the lay of the land, telling himself tomorrow would see him out. Go south to the catch basin; then it's not far to the tipi rings. How many ridges to cross between Gyp Creek and the catch basin? Took me a morning on two good legs, but shoot, I've already come some of that way.

That's what Clete would say. Shoot, it's a hop and a jump for a fellow like Sam . . . a fellow earning a vision name. Call him Running Moon after my granddad.

The boy's stomach flopped. "Clete," he said, "I'm not much of a runner now. Can't even walk. But if I get out of here . . . you just watch my tracks. It'll take plenty of sweat like you said, but I can be pretty good, I bet. Maybe." He sighed.

Dawn was slow coming among the heavy clouds. Sam crawled from his shelter as soon as shapes were visible on the slope. In the dim light, he bumped against the bare trunk of a dead juniper, which gave him an idea. If I can break it off, he thought, I'd have another cane.

Sam grabbed the trunk; his fingers just circled it. Testing, he pulled back on the tree. It felt slightly springy, not brittle-dead. Another pull cracked it at the base. He pumped the trunk back and forth to widen the split and wrench it loose.

With two supports, Sam swung his leg like a pendulum. It was easier than hopping, but it meant moving diagonally down the hill.

In the gray light, surfaces looked flat. Sam stumbled over small bumps that appeared level. The canes wedged in crevices he saw too late. There were no shadows in the draws or ravines. There was no morning sun. A chill, like a worry, made Sam look over his shoulder.

The night's juniper shelter seemed discouragingly

close. Beyond the juniper was the canyon he had followed. And beyond that the mountain of the vision site. Smoke-colored clouds hid the peak, but he was sure he knew the mountain.

Move on while I still have my bearings, he thought. If that's north, I'm heading south. Just follow my nose to the catch basin. He peered around for landmarks but found none. Cave in the Clouds would be a final checkpoint on this return trip. He started along the slope, hurrying. A distant rumble sounded in his ears like the opening gun of a race.

15

Sam had carried the dangling, pulsing ankle so far it seemed as much a part of him as aching lungs were a part of running. He picked goals—a spire of sage, a wild flower—and aimed for them.

He couldn't ignore his empty stomach. Even his legs and arms and chest felt hollow. He plucked a dry sprig of foxtail and stuck it in his mouth.

Lightning darted across the hills. It'll be a real storm when it gets here, he thought. He counted the seconds between the lightning flash and the thunder. Ten seconds

. . . it's two miles away but coming fast. There were flashes ahead, too. He leaned on his makeshift canes and swung his leg forward as quickly as he could.

He wondered if he might be drifting off course because of angling downhill. Won't matter, he decided. That catch basin was in a long gulch. Even if I'm a bit off, I'll see the water.

Another spurt of lightning. Five seconds. Thunder . . . one mile off. The air cooled and the breeze died. A rabbit scurried for cover in the dim light.

The rain began. It came quietly, pattering over the dry earth. When it reached Sam, he closed his eyes and welcomed the cool mist on his face. He caught drops on his palm and pressed them to his mouth.

Sam soon found the going slippery. The shale slid on top of the mud, putting him off-balance. His boot became clump-thick and heavy with gumbo; his hair was soaked and his jacket icy against his skin.

Within minutes the wind rose, blowing sheets of rain before it until a steady cascade walled around Sam. It slanted down gray on all sides. He made his way with head down, blinded by the rain. Move lower on the hill, he told himself, get out of the wind. Find shelter.

Sam hobbled down the open slope, one shoulder bent into the wind. He squinted ahead. Even so, he stumbled into a foot-deep washout, landing full-length in the mud.

Spitting and choking, he got to his knees. "Lousy ankle!" he cried, giddy with the pain. When he looked around at last, he realized with dismay, "I broke the cane." Must have fallen on it, he thought. Go on without the cane. A great mocking laugh bubbled up inside him, unexpected, choking.

"Well, Clete," he said, "got any suggestions? How about a funny story? Have you heard the one about the dumb kid that ran off . . . wanted to find power in the mountains . . . that one?" He choked again.

No, he thought, even Clete wouldn't think that was funny. Shoot, he'd say, the kid's pulled a boner this time, Sam has.

In the mud beside him, a tiny, moving form clung to a twig. Well, grasshopper, Sam thought, you're looking miserable, too. He reached out and wrapped his hand around the green insect and held it up to look closely at it. The large, unblinking, droopy eyes stared in return. The mouth worked defiantly to blow a single, dark-brown bubble.

"It's Clete and his tobacco," Sam said, giggling. "Come to give me power." The more he thought of it, the sillier the solemn grasshopper's face became. Sam rocked back and forth, laughing hysterically. "It's my spirit-helper grasshopper, come to give me power."

The laughing ended in a sob and he opened his hand. The hopper hesitated, unbelieving, and shot free into the mud again. Hopped again. Sam drew one hand over his forehead as if to clear it. Get away from here, he thought, find another cane. Don't I need another cane?

He forced his way against the storm, braced on the umbrella. The only tree he found was too scrawny for a windbreak. The only fallen limb was too rotten for a cane.

If I can see the catch basin from the next rise, he thought, then I'll know where I am. Even in this light, there'll be a reflection of the water.

But when he reached the crest, eyes squeezed against the rain, peering desperately along the meadowland, he did not find the landmark. How many ridges since the river? he wondered. I should have counted the first time so I'd know when I was close. Why didn't I? Was it two ridges? Three? Why didn't I pay attention?

The wind bellowed around him but brought no answers. "I'll try for the next ridge," he said aloud, although he did not know he spoke. His head seemed to be spinning.

Shivering, he made his way down the slope and across the wide meadow. Sometimes he forgot where he was going and why, but he kept hopping and the jolts kept him awake.

On the far hillside, his leg buckled, and he sagged to his knees with head bowed, rain peppering his bare neck. "Keep going," he said. "I'll see the catch basin . . . from this rise. . . . I will."

"I will!" Sam shouted through the wind. Who was that shouting? he wondered.

He forced his tired leg to carry him again. "A few more feet," he said. "Get to that rock there," and then "to that sage," and "one more jump. One more. One more."

Dully Sam glimpsed a cloud lifting from a dark peak ahead of him. I don't remember that peak, he thought in confusion, not by the catch basin.

The lightning flared across the sky some distance away. Storm's moving over, he told himself. It's light ahead of me . . . in the south. Be easy finding the catch basin if the rain stops. When I circle this peak, I'll see the water.

Grassland stretched away to grayness in the rain. It's big, Sam considered, be easy to miss a landmark in all this. Be easy to miss, said an echo in his mind.

"I'll find it," he said. "Around this hill, I'll see it." He'd come far enough, he was certain of it.

I won't look until I get around, he told himself. I just want to look down and see that water. I'm that close.

The rain felt lighter. Sam's spirit surged. It was half an hour before he worked his way to the far slope.

He looked up hopefully, but where he expected the catch basin, he saw a small hilltop. Beyond it and all around to his left were the dark, wet caps of grassy ridges. There was not even a puddle to mistake for the basin.

Sam looked to his right. No wonder, he thought, no wonder I didn't remember this peak by the basin. It's nowhere near the basin. I'm nowhere near it.

He toppled heavily onto the ground. A sense of aloneness, more painful than his ankle, pinned him there. His

chest felt raw. To relieve the ache inside, he hollered.
"Somebody help me!"

16

Am I going in a circle? he wondered desperately. I could
be anywhere.

He closed his eyes and his head bobbed forward. "Just
a little farther," he mumbled as if dreaming. He rolled
onto hands and knees to crawl forward. Sharp stones
under his battered knees woke him. "Was I going around
this mountain?" He lifted his dazed face.

A rocky ledge jutted out ahead. That far, he told himself, struggling up against the umbrella. He was a long
time between hops, rousing his strength.

After the ledge, he sighted on a dead, twisted tree
trunk. Hop, jolt, stop. If he was going in circles, he
would circle until he collapsed.

Keep moving, he thought, stay awake. If the clouds
lift, I'll get my bearings on the sunset. Must be about
sunset. Must be a day gone.

Sam squinted at the gray along the horizon. It was now
on his right. It was light in the south before, he puzzled,
or have I circled again?

Sam craned his head toward the mountain peak. He

stared. Where he expected one peak, he found two. They were massive boulders parted like the halves of a giant oyster shell. He tried to understand, but his head was spinning.

Then, sighting on a spruce, he hopped tediously on. When he looked up again, he found the opening between the boulders had changed into a slim needle's eye. He looked at it for some time. Finally, he whispered, "It's Cave in the Clouds."

How can it be? he wondered. He stretched for each idea, but they were like slippery toeholds. The Cave looked small when I first saw it, Sam realized, and now it's right over me. I'm miles off course. He sank down and buried his head in his hands, feeling the cold wind pressing, the steady pain.

Something sharp pricked his chest. He jammed his fingers into the jacket pocket, tugged out a small rock object and squinted at it in the dim light. It seemed to be a seashell. Where had it come from? He squeezed the rock to be sure it was real. He wanted to sleep, to slide into a shadowy, cold world. He was very cold. Just to sleep would be welcome.

Press the rock. Squeeze it. Feel it. Wake up. Stay awake. A rock, a seashell. From a mountain. Yes, that was right. It was from a mountain, one he had climbed . . . and fallen . . . yes, but where was he now?

I started south, he thought stubbornly. I know I did. He raised his face to the sky. Clouds tumbled before the wind, reflecting the light of sunset. The light was west all the time, Sam realized. I went west. So now what? He sat motionless.

If I go on south from the Cave, he thought at last, I should come out . . . maybe on that path to the tipi rings. Still he huddled in the wind, summoning strength. At least, Sam thought, I didn't go north into the next state like Mrs. Em said. At least I don't have that far to backtrack.

His head throbbed. There was something he had overlooked. He sensed it. Was it something Mrs. Em had said?

Lines of a map floated in his mind, but he couldn't focus on them. He vaguely imagined Mrs. Em drawing on the strip of blackboard.

"I'll make the map here," he said, taking up two stones in his hand. "Here's the catch basin and here's Cave in the Clouds." He marked them with the stones.

"Going north," Sam recited slowly, tracing a thin line with his forefinger, "I found Gyp Creek and followed along and turned west, and right up here was the vision site." He placed the fossil shell to fix the vision site.

No one ever found it there before, he thought. It washed out of the rocks just for me. A gift from the mountain. A shell as old as the hills. Older. Sam's head felt woozy. He held his arms wide. The circle of the world, he told himself. I can feel it. There's power like Clete said. I found it.

The map whirled before him. When it settled down,

he drew a wide diagonal line along the eastern side. "That's for Big Crow," he said in a loud voice to steady himself.

"And Little Crow was below the catch basin." He added a squiggly line. "I slept about here and saw the lights of Vista in this direction. And here's Mrs. Em's house." Picturing the small, snug house, a pup nesting on the rug, made his eyes sting.

"What else was on that map?" he persisted. "We came along the road here." He lined a road. "And we crossed the north-south county road." He added a short vertical. "And found the tipi rings." He made circles in the mud.

All around, the sunset made the peaks golden against the gray, departing storm. Sam saw only the distance between himself and the basin.

The map's too squatty, he thought. Mrs. Em's map was skinny north and south with that county road closer in. Not that it matters.

Sam caught his breath. Of course it matters! I didn't make the road as long as she did, either . . . and she said . . . Do it right. Move it over the way her map lay. The thing he'd tried to remember churned at the back of his mind. Do it right, he repeated. She put the county road about here, running north. And if I just draw it on north, up toward the next state, the way she said . . . why . . .

He couldn't believe his eyes. The road stretched up past Cave in the Clouds on the west. If Mrs. Em's map had had good proportions, Sam was closer to the road than to the catch basin. He hardly dared hope there might be a way out.

West, then. How far? Get my heading on the sun, he thought, stumbling up. He grabbed the shell stone and slipped it into his pocket for a lucky piece.

Sam hobbled toward the western slope. The gully below was in shadow. Hurrying, he tripped and fell. It reopened a cut on his knee, but he got to his feet, weaving back and forth.

Halfway through the gully, Sam grew sick and bewildered. Going where? he wondered. In the murky light, strange shapes and shadows surrounded him. Was that a bush? Or a bear? Were those waves or blowing branches? Where was he?

His ankle drooped low, raking over the rough ground, sending up new pain. It struck at the pit of his stomach until he retched. The slope swung before his eyes. He lost balance and fell headlong. Lying limp, he thought he saw a movement on the ridge.

A thin figure, a boy, ran along the rise. Sam smiled to watch him glide there, tall against the sky, like a daylong runner. An Indian boy has come to run with me, Sam thought. The boy raised his arms, whirled in a great loop and skimmed over the hill toward Sam.

I want to go with him, Sam thought. More than anything he wanted to run with the boy, to feel like himself again. Even to be a lonely boy seemed a welcome thing.

It's not lonely when I run, Sam thought, and that's a great mystery. Me . . . the great mystery. Strange way to think. Strange place to run! Who would run here? It's a crazy . . . wonderful thing to do and that boy dares to do it. Look how sure and proud he is.

"My running shoes," Sam mumbled, "where are they?" He groped about the muddy clumps. "Where are they?" He lifted his head. "Wait for me," he tried to call.

The boy raced as fleet and light as a mirage, shimmering, beckoning. I know that boy, Sam thought suddenly. It can't be!

Sam fought to get up. I'm all stove in, he thought, can't make the break. He sensed the runner draw near him. Stand over him. Reach out.

A touch both cold and electric shook Sam. One moment he felt fear; the next, as though the runner had charged him with power. "Do it," he mumbled, "kick it."

He crawled along the rocky slope to the ridge. Only the palest gray light lingered.

Before him the slope eased down to a lower ridge. Beyond was a wide flatland and Sam saw a steady, pale line: the road.

"It's there," he said, turning back to the runner. And he was amazed to find himself alone on the hillside.

"There was a runner here," he whispered. "I'm sure . . . a runner's spirit." He wouldn't leave me. He must still be here but I can't see him. His power's here. I can feel it.

Sam lurched over the uneven stretch of ground to the

lower ridge, barely visible in the darkness. About half a mile to that road, he thought. I'll get there on all fours if I have to. Someone will stop. Someone will.

While he watched, the red taillights of a car ran like twin beads along the pale path. Faintly, he heard the engine drone.

The slope down to the grassland was steep, and the earth was sticky from the rain, oozy to slide along. Sam inched downward, digging in his bootheel. Even so, he slid out of control and tumbled into a heap at the bottom. He hauled himself up, shivering.

Got to get warm, he thought, cold enough to freeze. His jacket had ripped open in the fall. I'll freeze, he repeated, even in summer. Be medical history if I don't move.

He fumbled for the umbrella-cane and turned toward the road, swaying as he stood. There were headlights now, a truck coming slowly. Above the headlights was a third light, aimed into the fields. Sam wondered if his eyes were playing tricks on him.

"Hey," he said, as though his voice could carry over the noise of an engine. The lights stopped. Had they seen him?

Instead the truck backed across the road and turned in the direction it had come. The taillights slipped away.

Sam hunched his shoulders against a rush of dizziness. His mind seemed to fly before him. He stumbled blindly forward, one hop and then another.

He had covered two-thirds of the distance when the truck with three lights appeared again. It seemed as unreachable as a plane passing overhead. He kept the pace of his slow hops.

Even as the shaft of light crawled nearer, Sam did not raise an arm or call out. He moved doggedly forward, too numb to care. He blinked when the spot beamed on his face, but he did not stop.

"Sam!" It was a woman's voice.

If he heard, he did not answer. Two silhouettes crossed the beam of light, like moths against a streetlamp.

"Sam!"

The boy wavered but went on. Perhaps he only imagined the figures coming toward him.

"I knew we were right to go looking," said a woman's voice. "I knew he'd figure out the road."

The man reached Sam first. For a moment the boy had the notion it was Clete, taller, brawnier.

The woman came up, puffing, holding her side. "Sam, you all right?"

Sam stared blankly at her. The flaring gray hair seemed familiar.

"The map . . ." he said. His words slurred as he slumped forward. His next impression was of being carried. There was a strong horsey scent about the man's jacket.

"Sprained ankle," Sam said thickly.

The man chuckled. "Your ankle's broke, son," said

his low rumbly voice. "But we'll get it fixed. You'll run again."

Sam's mind tumbled faster than he could reel it in. "Sprained," he insisted. "How . . . you know I run?"

"All my patients run," answered the man. "I'm a horse doctor." Sam felt him chuckle again. "Don't worry though, we won't have to shoot you."

They settled Sam in the middle of the truck cab. Mrs. Em tucked a wool jacket around him and patted his head onto her shoulder. "Hurry up, Doc. He's cold and he's hurt. Hurry."

"We got him," said the man. "Won't take but a few minutes to get to the hospital. He's as good as cured."

The cab was warm. Sam was as exhausted as he was dizzy. He closed his eyes. The jolting truck was the softest ride he could imagine.

Mixed up with a dream he heard the man ask "What was he doing in those hills?"

"He went up to that old vision site," said Mrs. Em. "I should have stopped it, seeing he didn't know the mountains. But he seemed to be working something out for himself and I didn't interfere. I should have."

"Well, he's out now," said Doc, "be good as new . . . and probably a lot smarter. How long ago did you say?"

"It's three days since he left my place. Should have been back in a day and a half. Who'd think we'd have such a storm? Lucky he didn't freeze."

"He's gonna be as hungry as a harvest crew."

Sam tried to speak.

"He's coming around," said Mrs. Em. "Have a sip of coffee from my thermos."

Sam dipped his head dutifully to the cup. The warm drink tasted fine.

"I found magic," he whispered to Mrs. Em. He reached into his pocket for the fossil. Instead he found the pocket ripped open and empty. "It's gone," he said unhappily.

"What's gone?" asked Mrs. Em. "Can't have lost much. You didn't have much."

"It had power," Sam said, "from the mountain. . . ." He was at a loss to explain. He had had the shell, he was certain of that. Held it in his hand. Hadn't it kept him awake when he needed help? It did have power, he thought stubbornly. And so did the runner. He couldn't clear his head properly to think. Was there a runner?

17

Bands of yellow light on a blue wall wavered before Sam's eyes when he woke up in the small hospital room. The sun beaming through venetian blinds had a late-afternoon tint. He wondered if he had slept a whole day; he certainly didn't remember much else.

The night before was a blur in his mind. Strange voices and faces and lights and smells and wrenching pain and then, blissfully, no pain. And sleep. And a dream he couldn't quite bring back . . . with a figure in it he tried to remember.

Turning his head, Sam noticed a glass jar filled with flowers, pink cosmos, on the nightstand beside his bed. Someone had been here and Sam knew who. He was smiling to himself when a head appeared around the edge of his door and Mrs. Em came into the room.

"Look at you," she said, "Rip Van Winkle awakes!" She dropped a parcel and a book onto the armchair beside the bed. Then she gathered up his hand and patted it energetically while she beamed at him.

"You were asleep before they finished putting on the cast last night . . . and again this morning when I came in . . . and at noon . . . and an hour ago. I brought you a chocolate malted milk earlier and had to drink it myself . . . and a vanilla one after that, which I also drank. I'd have brought you one now . . . but I was too full to take a chance."

"Sure sounds good," Sam said. It did. In fact he was ravenous.

"Let me get the nurse. They fed you with a tube, but there must be something else. Soup at least." Mrs. Em let go of his hand and stepped out of the room. She was back in a minute. "Coming right up," she said. "I promise a malt tonight so you can celebrate."

Mrs. Em looked closely at Sam's face. "I was right," she said. "You look ten times better. 'A good sleep will fix him up,' that's what I told your mother."

"My mother!" Sam wanted to pull the covers over his head. He couldn't face her. Was she coming? And how did Mrs. Em know?

"Oh, yes. There was a report on the six-o'clock news . . . about a missing boy. So I put one and one together and came up with a fearless history student. I telephoned her right away and told her not to worry. Course that was before the storm. Don't know what I would have said at that point."

Mrs. Em sat down on the red, vinyl armchair, which wheezed under her.

Sam turned his face away. "I never meant to be any trouble."

"Ah!" Mrs. Em waved his words away. "All's well that ends well. . . . I called her again and said I'd drive you home . . . assuming you'll ride that far with me. I told her you were fine and you'd most likely be released tomorrow or the next day."

"Was she very . . . what did she say?" After that long bus trip, Sam thought, to come home and find me gone. What will I say to her?

"She was some upset . . . you'd expect that, wouldn't you? But she asked me to tell you that she'd heard about Clete and she was sorry."

Sam nodded, but he didn't trust himself to speak. He

would make it up to her, he told himself. He wasn't just a dumb kid that ran out on her. First of all, there must be some work down at the stockyard, even with a broken ankle. He'd show her he was growing up. The dream stirred again at the back of his mind, but he still could not remember exactly . . . a figure, moving . . .

"How long before I can walk?" he asked, turning to Mrs. Em.

"You'll be on crutches for a few weeks and then you'll have a cane for a while. . . . Oh, you'll cut a dashing figure. Come to think of it, I have a cane I'll loan you. Belonged to my granddad and it's hand-carved. It's a real doozy!"

Sam laughed. "I wouldn't want to lose it."

"How can you lose it if you're leaning on it? You returned my umbrella, didn't you? Besides, it will give me a chance to see you again and hear about the rest of your summer. I haven't had so much excitement in years.

"This is much more interesting than the time Elroy Barnes built a raft and launched himself onto the Big Crow River. . . . Possibly we'd read too much Mark Twain that year. Anyway, his raft snagged on a log sticking out from a sandbar in the middle of the river. Lucky thing for Elroy, because he couldn't swim a stroke. Just fool luck got him onto that sandbar. It was hours before they found him. Was his dad boiling!" She laughed and shook her head. "Poor Elroy."

Sam managed a small smile. He didn't want to be another Elroy. He felt that something wonderful had happened . . . not counting the broken ankle. If only he could remember the figure that was teasing his mind . . . flitting out of reach . . . maybe it would explain.

"I brought you a book," Mrs. Em held it out, "to fill your spare time. I don't think it's dangerous reading material since you're through sailing for the summer."

Sailing? Sam frowned as he held up the book. "*Don* . . ." he began, staring at the strange name.

"*Don Quixote*," said Mrs. Em, "remember? We talked about him . . . the knight errant, looking for important causes. . . . It's an old book, but I'd like you to have it . . . because it's about a dreamer, which is a good thing to be. Especially if it gives you a good idea of yourself . . . and especially when you also do real things . . . like running. That must be quite a sport."

"Yes, it is," said Sam, trying to listen and remember at the same time. "You have to give it everything you've got."

"Oh, my," said Mrs. Em, ducking her head. "I'm sure you do that all right." She brushed quickly at the corner of her eye and seemed flustered until she spied the package in the chair beside her.

"Almost forgot. I brought along some clothes for you," she said. "Hope they'll fit. I went over to the Evanses'—they've got four boys—and said I needed some outgrown duds for a boy about so high and so wide." She held up a red plaid shirt and denims.

"Didn't want your mother to see how you really looked," she went on. "Got new underwear and socks and cleaned up your boot. We'll have to cut one pant leg to fit over the cast. When I tossed out your old, raggy clothes, this fell out of a pocket. Thought you might want it."

She put a stone in Sam's hand, and when he closed his fingers, it bit into his palm. It felt familiar. Quickly memories spilled into his mind. The climb. The sunlight on the mountaintops. The wide plains rolling like an ocean. The cold rain. And the runner. That was it: the figure waiting at the edge of his memory. A runner. A boy running proud along a ridgeline, free against the sky. It was as real as if it were happening again. Sam caught his breath with delight. It was his own dream, his vision, just as he'd hoped.

But when he opened his hand to look eagerly at the stone, there was nothing special about it that he could see. "I thought it was different," he said. "It seemed almost like a seashell, a magic shell, maybe. . . ." His voice dropped in embarrassment.

Mrs. Em leaned forward to study it. "Maybe it was," she said, "when you needed it to be. There's all manner of things in these mountains."

Sam looked at her in surprise. "That's what Clete said once. Said there were plenty of dreams and magic here. . . ."

"And he was right. Dreams and magic. Just what a boy needs."

Maybe the real magic shell was still in the mountains,

Sam thought, waiting on a hill for another boy who'd need it, same as the vision site. The image of the runner was strong in his mind now.

"Clete said when the old-time Indian boys went to the vision sites, they were looking for dreams to give them power . . . for when they grew up."

"Hmmmmmmm," said Mrs. Em agreeably. "I would say anyone who got himself and a broken ankle over six miles of mountains had plenty of power . . . and some magic thrown in. If you think that stone did it, then I say it's powerful."

"Not just the stone . . ." Sam began, "but a vision . . ." He hesitated putting it into words. Maybe he ought to think about it for a while first. Keep it part of his own special magic. She was watching him with her cool blue eyes. Waiting.

"There was a runner," he said slowly, "right up there in the hills with me. A boy . . . like me. I even thought it was me . . . running . . . somehow. . . . I don't know how. But he was so proud . . . and quick as a wild colt . . . and scrappy like the pup. He ran through the rain and the wind. Nothing stopped him. I don't think I could have gotten out . . . if it hadn't been for that boy. He just called up strength from the bottom of the barrel . . . the way a runner does."

Mrs. Em was silent for a time, staring toward the window. "That's a powerful dream to grow up with. I've always supposed that those Indian visions came out of stories and myths that were inside them all along. They believed in them and so they saw them. I suppose imagining . . . seeing a runner would be natural for you. It was inside you waiting. . . ."

"You don't believe there was a runner?" Sam sounded angry. He wished he'd kept the runner secret.

"I didn't say that," Mrs. Em said quickly. "But it's curious that the Indian boys found visions . . . animals and such . . . in the shapes of their legends . . . and your vision was mostly like yourself. As if you were looking for yourself."

Sam frowned. He didn't know what to make of that.

"But that's what a quest is," she went on, "a search. Some people take a lifetime and some never even begin. I'd say your vision was a fine beginning." She smiled at Sam. "Trust a youngster to do it right."

"I thought the runner was very brave," said Sam.

"He was," said Mrs. Em, "and he was gallant."

"It's like having something to live up to . . . finally . . . something to live up to."

"Oh, my," Mrs. Em repeated, brushing at her eyes again. "Well! Ah . . . let me have the book. We can begin it together."

Sam held it out, smiling. He felt as sure and happy as a runner. He thought he could face anything. The old heaviness was gone. Even his ankle would soon be strong again.

Mrs. Em slid back in the chair, curling her legs under

her, settling in, as she opened the book. "In a village of La Mancha . . ."

And Sam lay back against the pillows, with his hands nested under his head and his eyes fixed on her craggy, old face. He didn't want to miss a word.

Format by Joyce Hopkins
Set in Vail-Ballou Press, Inc.
HARPER & ROW, PUBLISHERS, INC.